★ RUBY ★ STARR ★

THE
GREAT MUSEUM
MiX-UP

AND OTHER
SURPRiSE
ENDiNGS

Also by Deborah Lytton

Ruby Starr

*The Fantastic Library Rescue
and Other Major Plot Twists*

RUBY ★ STARR ★

THE GREAT MUSEUM MiX-UP

AND OTHER SURPRISE ENDINGS

DeBORaH LYtTON

sourcebooks
jabberwocky

Published by Sourcebooks Jabberwocky, an imprint of Sourcebooks, Inc.
P.O. Box 4410, Naperville, Illinois 60567-4410
(630) 961-3900
Fax: (630) 961-2168
sourcebooks.com

Library of Congress Cataloging-in-Publication Data

Names: Lytton, Deborah A., author.
Title: The great museum mix-up and other surprise endings / by Deborah Lytton.
Description: Naperville, Ill. : Sourcebooks Jabberwocky, [2019] | Series: Ruby Starr ;
[3] | Summary: Ruby and the members of her lunchtime book club are thrilled when
the class field trip to the museum gives them the chance to follow in the footsteps of
an adventurer who may have discovered the last unicorn.
Identifiers: LCCN 2018033549 | (trade pbk. : alk. paper)
Subjects: | CYAC: Museums--Fiction. | School field trips--Fiction. | Friendship--
Fiction. | Books and reading--Fiction. | Clubs--Fiction. | Imagination--Fiction.
Classification: LCC PZ7.L9959 Gr 2019 | DDC [Fic]--dc23 LC record available at
https://lccn.loc.gov/2018033549

Source of Production: Berryville Graphics, Inc., Berryville, Virginia, United States
Date of Production: December 2018
Run Number: 5013841

Printed and bound in the United States of America.
BVG 10 9 8 7 6 5 4 3 2 1

For my mom, who always believes in me
With love

CHAPTER 1

How an Adventure Begins

Once upon a time, there lived a girl named Ruby Starr. (That's me.) In case we haven't met before, there are a few things you should know. If we *have* met before, see if you spot anything new.

1. I love, love, absolutely love books (every kind of book, especially the classics).
2. I have four besties: Siri, Jessica, Daisy, and Charlotte (plus a most-of-the-time friend named Will P).
3. I started the Unicorn Book Club with

my friends so we could read together and talk about books. In my opinion, the next best thing to reading a book is talking about a book.

4. I am really good at these things: writing, singing, and baking (but I still can't crack an egg using only one hand).

5. My dream is to one day be a famous author and to have so many published books that they take up an entire shelf in the library.

6. Sometimes I imagine I am in the pages of a book. My thoughts sort of fly up into bubble-gum bubbles full of ideas.

7. I believe in the power of imagination.

Today is Book Club Tuesday, so I am sitting at my usual lunch table with the other Unicorns discussing our latest read, which, this week, is *From the Mixed-Up Files of Mrs. Basil E. Frankweiler* by E. L. Konigsburg. (Fun book fact: This novel won the Newbery Medal in 1968 and has been considered a classic ever since. When I am a famous author, I hope to win *at least* one Newbery Medal for my work.)

"Has anyone finished the book?" I ask the Unicorns. Siri, Jessica, and Daisy are sitting across from me, and Charlotte is sitting to my right. My most-of-the-time friend, Will P, is sitting at the other end of the table with his book club, the Polar Bears. Sometimes I read with them too. Other times, I stay away from his friends because of their habit of throwing food.

"I finished the book in one day," Jessica announces. She is a super-speedy reader.

"It took me six days," Daisy admits. "But I'm done too."

"Same here," says Siri.

"Ruby and I finished on Saturday," Charlotte shares with a quick smile in my direction. Charlotte didn't like books when she first came to our school a few months ago. But that's different now.

"Excellent news. If everyone is finished, then we can begin our discussion," I say in my fake British accent. Certain words sound more official when I say them with an accent. *Discussion* is one of those words. Other words that are especially impressive in an accent are *s'mores, periwinkle,* and *brilliant.*

I have laid out a cloth napkin in the middle of the table for our lunches. On Book Club Tuesday, it is especially important to bring yummy snacks for sharing and also to wear something in the Unicorn's signature color, pink. I'm wearing a pink-and-white-striped T-shirt. Charlotte is wearing a pink cardigan over her red dress. Siri has her hair braided with pink ribbons, and Jessica and Daisy are wearing matching pink sweatshirts.

"Why do you think Claudia ran away to the

Metropolitan Museum of Art?" I ask as I hold up a small container of apple slices. Charlotte and Daisy each take one.

"She wanted an adventure," Jessica answers before she bites into a mini blueberry muffin.

"Claudia thought her family didn't appreciate her," Siri adds.

"Would you have run away?" Charlotte asks Siri. She offers us animal crackers. I choose a tiger.

Siri doesn't even take a moment to think before answering, "For sure."

"I think Claudia was good at planning," Daisy says, joining in the discussion. "She figured out how to eat, sleep in a bed, wash her clothes, and even take baths while living in a museum."

Then it's Siri's turn to ask a question. "If you did run away, would you want to run away to a museum?"

Daisy scrunches up her nose. "I wouldn't like to be there in the dark. It sounds creepy."

I nod. "I would bring a flashlight, so I could see everything. What about you, Jessica?"

"I would rather run away to a bookstore," she says with a big sigh. "Then I could read all the time, and no one would tell me to turn off the light and go to sleep."

Everyone laughs at that. We all know what it's like when you want to read just one more page and your parents turn off the light. (Secret factoid about me: sometimes I hide under the covers with a flashlight and keep reading even though I am supposed to be sleeping.)

"I would run away to the San Francisco Ballet," Charlotte tells us. "Imagine being part of a real ballet company." Charlotte stands up and spins around three times like it's an exclamation point at the end of her sentence.

I grin at my dancing friend. "I can't imagine being part of a ballet company. I can't even imagine taking a ballet class." My friends know that dancing is not my thing. Not at all! So smiles appear on all of our faces, starting from one side of the Unicorns and going to the other.

That's when I notice that something isn't right with Siri.

I've read a lot of Nancy Drew mysteries, and Nancy is always paying attention to little details. I'm sort of like a Nancy Drew in training. That's why I realize Siri isn't smiling her real smile. She has her worried expression on. It's the one where her eyebrows go down a little and her eyes get really big. I know this because she has been my best friend since kindergarten. I've seen her excited, worried, and even really mad. We've had sleepovers together and real adventures and even a few fights (which I would rather not think about). When you know someone as well as I know Siri, you can almost always tell what they are thinking—not that I have the power to read minds, although sometimes I wish I did.

I am a famous detective who can solve even the most complicated mystery because of my incredible mind reading abilities. I am interviewing three suspects accused of stealing a giant green diamond from a museum in New York. I ask all three where the diamond is and then read their minds. The first suspect is an old woman, who is thinking about her calico cat. The second suspect is a teenager, who is thinking about eating pizza with pineapple and pepperoni. The third suspect is the manager of the museum. He is thinking about the diamond hidden in his hat. Hey, I did it! I solved the crime!

I'm sure mind reading would have its downsides though—like reading minds you didn't actually want to read, but your power made you do it anyway. Here are three minds I would not like to read:

1. Will B (the other Will in our class, who has a habit of eating things you shouldn't eat, like pencil erasers and things that come from inside his nose).
2. A substitute teacher we had once named Mrs. Cheer, who was anything but cheery.
3. My brother Connor, who loves insects. I wouldn't want spiders and ants crawling around in my mind.

Anyway, I don't have to read minds to know that Siri and I are going to be friends forever. I give my best friend one of my signature winks and say, "I bet you would like to run away to a fabric store."

That gets me a teeny real smile. "Would there be a sewing machine there?"

I nod and answer her in my fake British accent. "Most definitely."

Siri offers me a piece of sushi. "I bet Claudia and Jamie got in a lot of trouble after they went home. The book doesn't show us that part of the story."

I'm growing to like cucumber rolls these days. I take the piece of seaweed, rice, and cucumber and give her some stick pretzels.

"I would get in a lot of trouble," I answer. It would be super-serious Trouble with a capital *T* (which would be a lot worse than my usual trouble with a lowercase *t*).

"Me too," Jessica agrees.

I think about this. "It might be worth it

though to solve a giant mystery like the one about Angel."

"Is there a statue at school with a mysterious past?" Charlotte asks us. She is still sort of new here. The rest of us have been together at this same school since kindergarten.

I shake my head. "Not that I know of, unless you want to investigate the lunch meat that is probably going to fly over here any minute." I point to the other end of the table where, right on schedule, Will P's friends have started flinging half-eaten sandwiches, chips, and everything in between.

Daisy scrunches up her nose. "We better clean up fast today."

We all put our containers into our lunch bags, and I shake out Mom's napkin before folding it up.

Siri hands me my water bottle. "We didn't get to choose a book for next week," she reminds us.

Jessica stands up just in time to avoid a

splatter of orange slice on her seat. "We'll have to vote on a new book tomorrow. Let's go to the swings."

I am just turning to follow Siri and Charlotte when it happens. It's worse than being fake vomited on (which has happened before), and it's worse than having a half-eaten, very slimy piece of salami hit my hand (which has also happened before). What happens is so awful it almost can't be described. But it happens to me.

Something lands in my hair!

I carefully reach my hand up to the spot just over my right ear... It's gooey. I am really afraid to see what it is. *Please don't let it be a meatball. Please don't let it be tuna fish.*

I pull the unidentified mush out of my hair, and there it is. Only guess what. I can't tell what it is!

My detective skills are pretty good, so I begin with the color. It's yellow. Then I look at the texture. It's sticky. I know it has to be in the food category, since it's lunchtime. That leaves a few options: It could be mango. It could be papaya. It could even be bell pepper.

I have to pause my detective work for a second. Because I have to do this:

EWWWWWWWWWWWWWWWWWWWWW!

"Sorry about that, Ruby." Will B is standing next to me.

"Is this yours?" I lift my hand up, so he can see the mush.

Will B nods. "I didn't mean for it to hit you. I was aiming for Bryden."

I want to say a lot of things right now. But most of them would probably get me into Trouble with a capital *T*. I also want to put this yellow mush into Will's sweatshirt pocket. But that would most definitely get me into Trouble with a capital *T*. So instead, I say this: "What is it?"

"I'm not sure. I think it's papaya. Or it could be mango."

If he doesn't know, that must mean he didn't eat it before he threw it. Which is better. I think.

"That explains a lot," I tell him as I turn away and drop the sticky goo into the nearest trash.

Siri is standing a few steps away from me. "What happened?"

I shrug. "What else? Flying food. I'm going to the bathroom to check out the damage."

"I'll come with you. What are besties for?" she says as she puts her arm around my shoulder.

Having a bestie is one of those things you don't realize is that important until you don't have one. Then you find out just how important it really is. There was a time when Siri and I were experiencing what my mom calls "friend troubles." I had more tears and stomachaches than I've had in probably my whole entire life. But all that is behind us now and we are closer than we have ever been, which is why I ask her this: "What's wrong?"

She shrugs. Shrugging is Siri's signature move. "Nothing." Only the worried expression is still on her face. Have you ever noticed that when someone doesn't want to tell you something, their face tells you anyway? Siri's face is telling me that something is very, very wrong.

"You can always talk to me, you know," I say in my brightest voice. "I'm really good at figuring things out." I am a whiz at word searches and guessing games. Here are my go-to choices for the animal guessing game that my family plays on long car rides:

1. Anteater
2. Porcupine
3. Toucan

"I know," Siri answers me. But she doesn't say anything else.

I have read stories where someone keeps

a secret and the secret ends up causing lots of problems for everyone, especially the hero. I hope this is not going to turn out that way.

Siri stays with me the whole time I wash the yellow goo out of my hair. She even stands next to me while I lean underneath the hand dryer to blow the side of my hair dry.

I imagine Siri and I are riding a golden dragonfly through a
garden of magical flowers. We are searching for the purple
praying mantis: the guardian of the magical story stone.
Whoever holds the stone knows all the stories in the world.
Siri spots the praying mantis underneath a ruby rose. He will
only tell us where the stone is hidden if we tell him a story
that makes him smile. Siri and I tell him about our friendship.
The praying mantis smiles and even winks. Then he hands
me the story stone. He is counting on us to keep it safe.

CHAPTER 2

The Best Assignment Ever (Really!)

O ur teacher, Mrs. Sablinsky, is all business after lunch. "Room 15, no dillydallying, please. Take your seats," she says as she claps her hands together. "We have a busy afternoon ahead of us." If I were a teacher, I would understand that sometimes students need to take their time. Maybe they are in the middle of writing a story in their imagination. (Everyone knows you can't rush a writer!)

I cut my imagination story short and hurry to my desk in the middle of the room. Last week, we moved to new seats, and I'm not sitting in the front near Jason anymore. He sleeps through class most of the time, so he's not the worst seat partner, but I can't say I enjoyed it. Now I am sitting near my friends, which is the best thing ever. Siri is to my right and Will P is to my left. Jessica is in front of me. Daisy is next to her and Charlotte is in the desk right behind me.

Mrs. Sablinsky sits in her director's chair in the front of the room. "I have a very exciting announcement for you. For the next two weeks, you will be working on a book report."

When Mrs. S says the magic word *book*, my ears perk up right away, like my dog, Abe, when he hears kibble being poured into his bowl. I already know this will be a better-than-best assignment. Our last assignment was a math report on creative ways to use numbers in everyday life. I wrote the paper about baking because I'm pretty much an expert at baking, and because numbers are super important when measuring ingredients. I know this from personal experience (but that's a whole other story).

I'm so happy that I turn and share a grin

with Siri right away. Jessica even claps for this news. But some students groan. Not everyone loves books and reading as much as I do.

"Let's keep the comments to ourselves," Mrs. S says with a little frown. "You will begin with reading a nonfiction book. You must choose a book about the natural world. This can include animals, plants, rocks, and insects. I have scheduled library time for tomorrow, so you can search for a topic that interests you. I will need to approve your title, as it must be at least one hundred pages long and nonfiction." Mrs. S smiles at me then. She knows that I love reading and that I want to be a writer when I grow up.

We used to have a problem understanding each other, but all that changed a few weeks ago. I'd give the credit to my pickle cupcake for bonding us, except I think it was more than that. It was like we were introduced for the first time. Sometimes when my brothers Connor and Sam argue over a game of chess or even what to watch on television, my mom tells them to start over, which is Mom Code for "Stop fighting and rewind so you can begin again." I think that's what happened to Mrs. Sablinsky and me. We started over.

I imagine I am in a world made of food. I stand on a
mountain covered in frosting with coconut sprinkles. Far
in the distance, I can see Mrs. Sablinsky standing on a
mountain covered with chocolate and cherries. We are
so very far apart. When a giant gummy bear shakes her
mountain and cherries start tumbling down, I run to the edge
to help. That's when I see the bridge between the mountains.
It is made entirely of pickle slices. I start across the bridge,
but one of the pickle slices slips loose and falls into the
river of caramel far, far below. Before I fall too, I leap to the
next slice and then hurry the rest of the way to save Mrs.
Sablinsky and bring her to safety.

"Ruby, do you have a question?" Mrs. Sablinsky asks.

I realize that she is not on the bridge with me but in the classroom—and I am waving my arms in the air to keep my balance. Except that I am sitting in my seat in the middle of the room. And everyone has a supergood view of me. Oops. Sometimes my imagination gets me into some marshmallow-sticky situations.

Mrs. Sablinsky is waiting for me to say something (and everyone else is staring!), so I hurry to think of a question really fast. "What time are we going to the library tomorrow?"

My teacher sighs. I do have that effect on her. But at least she didn't make her I-am-not-amused face. I have to admit, sometimes I come up with some really oddball questions. I have asked things like, "What time is it in Paris?" and "Why does the school ring a bell instead of banging a gong?"

Mrs. Sablinsky answers my question, even though it seems like she would rather not: "I have arranged for us to have library time tomorrow morning at nine o'clock."

I am so happy that I completely forget about my embarrassing arms-waving-in-the-air moment. The library is one of my absolute favorite places. Jessica turns around in her seat to grin at me. She loves books as much as I do. Her ponytail swishes across my desk as she turns back to face the front of the room. (Ruby fact: My ponytails never swish. They bounce.)

"Part two of the assignment is writing the book report." Groans around the room again. For some students, the next-worse thing to reading a book is writing about reading the book. For me, this is still in the best-assignment-ever category. Mrs. Sablinsky hands Will P a stack of papers. "Can you please help me pass these out to everyone?"

I bet if you took a poll of the class, mapped the answers out on a graph, and then turned the graph numbers into percentages, you would find that Will P passes out papers and gets to bring notes to the office more than any of the other students combined. Not that I'm jealous or anything. I'm not. I'm just making an observation. That's all.

Will P is known for his supercool red glasses and his signature sock collection. Today, he is wearing socks with numbers all over them. Will never seems to wear the same pair of socks twice. Also, he doesn't seem to have a problem matching up pairs. In my house, mismatched socks are the norm. Right now, I am wearing a sock with pink hearts on one foot and a sock with a dancing gorilla on the other foot. (The good thing is that no one except me knows because my green sneakers and pink laces cover the designs.)

I imagine I am on the Island of Unmatched Socks. This is
where all the missing socks go when they disappear from
laundry baskets and clothes dryers. The socks are all stacked
up in giant piles like hills. There must be more than a million
socks here. There are striped ones and white ones and even
some with patterns like stars. I start sorting through the
largest stack. After looking through hundreds that don't
belong to me, I find my missing dancing-gorilla sock. I even
find my sock that has a pig on it that looks like a cow. I will
never wear mismatched socks again!

"Ruby." Will P is calling my name. I'm not on the Island of Unmatched Socks. I'm here at school. "Here you go." He hands me the assignment.

"Thanks, Will," I say as I set the paper on my desk. Then I pretend to tie my shoelaces so I can get a peek at the dancing gorilla and pink hearts. Yep, definitely not matching!

Mrs. Sablinsky moves to the middle of the room and stands right near my desk. "I am giving each of you a copy of the assignment so there is no confusion. On the back, you will see the exact format I would like you to use for your final paper. You will need to come up with one topic from the book that you would like to share. Then you will use facts from the book to explain the topic."

She holds up a finished book report. "This is an example from one of my students last year. She did her report on horses—specifically, the way they arrived in North America." There is a really fancy drawing of a horse on the front cover of the report. The rest is typed. That's a good thing, because I'm way better at typing than writing by hand.

We get to see a few more examples after that. Mrs. S even passes them around the room, so we can look through them if we want. One of the reports is about dinosaurs, and another is about roaches. The roaches report is something my brother Connor would write. It's all about how strong the bugs are and how we can learn from them. Ewwwwww. I pass the paper on to Jessica really fast. She practically drops it on the floor as she flings it over to Daisy.

After that, we get time to finish our math homework. We are working on graphing, which actually isn't so bad, considering that it's math. Lucky for me, I solve the last problem just as the bell rings.

My heart skips a little bit when I see my grandma waiting for me in front of school. On the days my mom stays late at work, Gram is on pickup duty for me and my brothers, Sam and Connor. One of the things I love about Gram: she is always on time. She can't stand lateness. I guess everyone has something that bothers them. I don't have a problem with people being late, but I can't stand it when someone tells me the ending of a book before I have read it. If I were a teacher, I would write my own Book Rules that every student would have to follow.

MISS STARR'S
BOOK RULES

1. Never tell someone the ending of the book before they have read it.
2. Remember, characters are real to readers.
3. Always read the book before seeing the movie.

I am no longer me. I am Miss Starr, Teacher Extraordinaire. My classroom doesn't look like an ordinary classroom with rows of desks and boards around the room. Instead, my classroom looks like a library. There are shelves of books weaving around the room in a maze pattern so books have to be discovered. My students are gnomes in super-trendy clothes. On the first day of class, I teach them my Book Rules. The most important three rules are:

1. Never tell someone the ending of a book before they have read it for themselves.

2. Remember that characters in books are real to readers and to authors.

3. Always read a book before seeing the movie version.

"Hi, pumpkin. How was your book club today?" Gram asks as she gives me a hug.

Wait a minute, what is Gram doing in my magical library classroom?

Answer: she's not in my magical library classroom. The imagination bubble fades as I greet my grandma. "We had to cut the meeting short on account of a food fight at the other end of the table. Oh, and a mushy something landed in my hair."

"I'm so sorry, sweetie pie." Gram smooths my curls back from my face. I can tell she is looking for leftovers.

"I think we are going to try sitting at a different lunch table from now on."

"Now that sounds like a very good idea," Gram says. She takes my backpack and slings it over her shoulder, just as she always does. I am definitely one of those people who prefers when things are the same. I like to know what to expect— for instance, Gram wearing my backpack to the car. I don't like when things go and change on me right when I get used to them. In a lot of books, things change so the characters can learn from new situations. This is one of those things that I enjoy reading about way more than experiencing.

Gram and I walk side by side through the parking lot. She puts her arm around me. "Are you in the mood for ice cream?"

"I am always in the mood for ice cream!"

"Then climb into my sleigh, and away we will go." Gram waves her hand in front of her car like a magician, but I know she is really just unlocking the door with the button on her key.

Gram's car is known as Grambus. It's not really a bus—it's Gram's white SUV with a license plate that says GRAMBUS. Also, Gram's car wears a costume for every season. Since it's December, Grambus is wearing a pair of reindeer antlers on the hood and a big, red Rudolph nose on the front bumper.

I get into the back seat and buckle up. Gram and I have just enough time before we pick up my brothers to do special outings, like a visit to the library or going to my favorite ice cream shop, Ice Cream Heaven.

If you haven't been to Ice Cream Heaven before, it's this cuter-than-cute ice cream shop where the entire place is decorated in a sky theme, with blue walls and clouds everywhere. The ice cream comes in little clear-pink bowls, and the spoons start out as pink, but they change to purple when they get cold, which is so cool.

I hurry to the counter to look for my favorite flavor: chocolate chip caramel. But my eyes get sidetracked when I notice a sign—FLAVOR OF THE MONTH: *UNICORN*. The ice cream is light pink with little, curly sprinkles dancing around in shades of yellow, blue, and white. It looks delicious.

A *whoosh* of excitement flies through me like a bright-orange dragonfly. OK, I know people besides me and my friends like unicorns. I mean, everyone probably likes unicorns, right? What's not to like about a magical animal that looks like a horse but has a swivel horn and makes an appearance in all the best books? But somehow, at this moment, it seems like the Flavor of the Month was created especially for me. Plus, it gives me a better-than-best idea about my new book report.

Which is why, without even trying a taste of the flavor, I completely abandon my signature ice cream. "May I have a scoop of unicorn ice cream with cloud topping?" I ask my grandma.

Her blond eyebrows rise up in surprise. "Instead of the usual? Well, if that's the case, I will try something new myself."

"Could I have a taste of the peach sunrise sorbet please?" Gram asks the girl behind the counter. But instead of trying it herself, Gram hands the tasting spoon to me. "Let me know if you think I should order this one today."

The little spoon has a bite of pale-orange sorbet on it. I taste it. Yum.

I grin at Gram. "Most definitely."

"A scoop of peach sunrise it is, then."

After Gram pays for our ice cream, we find an empty gold table and sit down together. I pull out my spoon to check. Yep, it's already turning from pink to purple. Then I take a bite of the unicorn ice cream.

"Well, how is it?" Gram asks me. She is waiting for my official verdict. I'm like a judge on *Cupcake Champions* (a cupcake baking show my brother Sam and I love to watch).

Mmmmmmmmmmmmmmmmmmm!

It tastes even better than it looks. I decide to give her my opinion using my fake British accent. It sounds way more professional than my regular voice. "I would say that it is a splendid combination of sweet and tart that reminds me of strawberry lemonade. Absolutely brilliant." My accent is pretty good, if I do say so myself. I've read a lot of books by British authors, so that helps.

"Then I'm glad we came here today." Gram reaches over to give my hand a little squeeze. "So, tell me all about school."

I take another bite of my ice cream before launching into the details in my regular voice. "This week the Unicorns are reading *From the Mixed-Up Files of Mrs. Basil E. Frankweiler.*"

"Oh, I remember your mother loved that book when she was young."

I nod. "There was a lot to discuss. Only Siri seemed sort of sad today. I asked her if everything was OK, and she said it was, but it seemed like maybe she wasn't telling me the truth."

Gram takes a spoonful of her sorbet. Then she says, "Sometimes being a good friend means being patient. When Siri is ready to talk, she will know where to find you."

Gram always has the very best advice. She's

right—when Siri is ready to talk, I will be there to listen. I just hope she's ready to talk soon, because misunderstandings between friends can really take a story in the wrong direction. (I know this from personal experience.)

"Have you thought about what you're making for my cookie party?" Gram asks. Every year, my grandma has a party where she invites family and friends to bring cookies to share. No one wants to bring an ordinary cookie, no matter how tasty it is. So each year, the cookies get more and more creative.

"Sam and I want to make something together. We haven't decided what to bake yet. Mom is making her famous chocolate chip cookies." (Factoid: my mom makes the world's best chocolate chip cookies. Really and truly!)

"After your pickle cupcakes, I'm expecting something very unusual." Gram winks at me. I know she doesn't really like the idea of nontraditional flavors, but the wonderful thing about Gram is that she'll support my ideas anyway. "It's time to go get your brothers," she says as she takes our empty pink bowls to the recycle bin. "On the way, I'll tell you about how George managed to eat your grandfather's entire plate of spaghetti last night."

I laugh as I walk with my grandmother to the parking lot where Grambus is waiting. I love hearing my grandma's stories about Abe's dog-brother George and the messes he makes at my grandparents' house. I can't even imagine what life would be like if we had adopted George instead of Abe!

My family is sitting around the dinner table eating pasta.
George, who looks just like Abe but is way more of a
troublemaker, is sitting underneath the table just like Abe
does when he waits for morsels to drop onto the floor. Except
George doesn't like to wait. Instead, he bounces up and down,
tilting the table left and right. The plates slip right off the
edges, and George slurps up the pasta before the dishes crash
to the ground. We try to catch the plates but end up slipping
around in the pasta sauce that is now all over the floor. Sam
and Connor grab for me as I slide into Mom. Dad reaches for
Mom just as we crash into her. All five of us land in a heap.
George happily licks our faces.

CHAPTER 3

Unicorns Are Real, Aren't They?

On Wednesday morning, at exactly 8:55 a.m., Mrs. Sablinsky rings the little bell on her desk.

"Please finish up and put away your journals. We are heading to the library in five minutes to choose your books for the new assignment."

I am right in the middle of a journal entry about my friendship with Siri, so I finish the last sentence. It says:

Siri and I even have plans to go to the same college in New York City and then live together in a very cool apartment, where she will have a fashion studio, and I will write my novels.

I draw a picture of a book next to the last word. Drawing books wherever and whenever possible is my new thing. I'm getting really good at it. My sketch looks like this:

Then I put away my journal and my favorite green pencil. Will P is just putting away his journal too. We are usually the last two students to finish creative writing.

"I'm thinking about a report on dinosaurs or polar bears," Will P tells me. "So I prepared for both." He points to his dinosaur socks.

I don't spot any polar bears on the socks—just raptors, a Tyrannosaurus rex, a Brontosaurus, and a Triceratops. (I know. I am sort of an unofficial dinosaur expert on account of my brother Connor.) Dinosaurs and polar bears are not the same species, unless there is something I don't know. "Um, I'm pretty sure those are just dino socks."

"Not exactly," he says. He leans over and rolls the dinosaur socks down. He is wearing his polar bear socks underneath his dinosaur socks.

"Now that is impressive." I grin at Will. What he doesn't know is that seeing not one but two pairs of matching socks really amazes me—probably even more than his matching the socks with possible book topics. I decide to share my wonderful idea for a book report subject with Will. I take a big breath. "I'm searching for a unicorn book."

"Unicorns?" His face squelches up the way it does when he can't figure out the answer to a math problem (which has actually only happened once). "But they're not real."

"I would have to disagree with that

statement." I cross my arms in front of me and stand up a little taller. "Unicorns *are* real."

Will pushes his red glasses higher on his nose and then crosses his arms exactly like mine. He isn't giving up on this. "Have you ever seen one?"

I am not budging either. Sometimes the best way to answer a question is with another question. "Have you ever seen a dinosaur?"

Will shakes his head. "Dinosaurs are extinct."

I turn his argument around on him. "If dinosaurs are extinct, then why can't you say the same thing about unicorns?" OK, I might be a tad touchy about this topic. This isn't the first time someone has told me that unicorns aren't real. And it really, really bothers me. *A lot.*

Will doesn't say anything. *Uh-oh, not again,* I think. The last time this happened, Will and I almost stopped being friends. Well, actually, we *did* technically stop being friends, but only for one week, and only until I apologized.

Before I have to say something to fill the silence, Will throws his hands in the air. "Good point, Ruby. I never thought of it that way before."

Winning an argument is a pretty great feeling, I have to admit. Winning an argument against the smartest boy in the entire fifth grade, well, that is beyond great. It's *stupendiferous*, to use a Will P term.

I don't have time to bask in the win though, because at that exact moment, Will's friends Bryden and Will B stop by our desks. These are probably my two least favorite people in our whole school because:

1. They start the horrific food fights and usually hit me with flying, half-eaten luncheon meats.
2. They think super-gross things are funny.

Before I can make a quick getaway (where is my invisible race car when I need it?), I am surrounded. Bryden is on my left eating something that looks like a burrito but smells like tuna fish. It makes my stomach flip upside down. Will B is on my right stretching a rubber band back and forth, which I am pretty sure is going to snap into my arm any second.

"OK, well, I'll see you in the library," I mutter and back away as quickly as possible, avoiding the tuna burrito and the rubber band.

My friends are waiting for me just outside the classroom door. The Unicorns walk together to the library. Jessica tells us about her plans to visit relatives in Japan next summer.

"My mom made the reservations last night. We'll be on the airplane for eleven and a half hours," she says.

Charlotte's eyes get really big just thinking about it. "That's almost half a day!"

Daisy turns around, so she is walking backward in front of us. "I thought a two-hour car ride was long. What will you do for that many hours?"

Jessica braids her hair as she walks. "My sister is going to watch movies. She says she can probably see six in a row."

"You'll have to bring a lot of books with you," I tell her.

"And a pillow," Siri adds. Everyone laughs at that because we all know how much Siri likes to sleep.

Mrs. Sablinsky is holding open the red door that leads to our library. The Unicorns are the only students left outside. She says to us, "Less talking and more walking, please."

We all look at each other and then, at the same time, start run-walking to the door. (Factoid: run-walking is that half run, half walk that you do when someone is waiting for you and you need to get there quicker than you can by just walking.

It would also be useful if you had just eaten all the honey-raisin granola in a bear's house and were trying to escape without drawing attention to yourself, because the bear would certainly notice if you sprinted, but might not be suspicious of someone run-walking through the forest.)

We pass by Mrs. S without slowing and zoom right into the library. Mrs. Xia, the librarian, is sitting at the front desk, so I zip over to say hello while my friends start looking for books. Mrs. Xia is one of my absolute favorite people. I will miss her next year when I go to middle school. I hope the librarian there will love books as much as Mrs. Xia loves them.

"Good morning, Ruby. I have something for you." She hands me a sticker that reads, in yellow letters, Turn the Page. Underneath the words is a drawing of a mouse reading a book.

I put the sticker on my blue sweater right away. "Thank you. Have you ever noticed that mice are characters in so many books, but most people are super scared of them in real life?"

Mrs. Xia chuckles at that. "I'm sorry to tell you I am one of those people."

I nod. "Me too," I whisper.

Then Mrs. Xia gets down to business. She always asks me the same question when I come to the library, but my answer is always different. Here is the question: "What are you reading right now?"

I answer her with the title of this week's book club read. "We just finished *From the Mixed-Up Files of Mrs. Basil E. Frankweiler*. Mrs. Sablinsky loaned us copies. It's one of her favorites."

Mrs. Xia's eyes shine with excitement as she claps her hands together. "One of my favorites too. I have always dreamed of staying in a museum overnight." She comes around the desk to stand next to me. "Do you need any help today?"

"Actually, I do." I can see my friends

disappearing into the stacks of books. "I am looking for a book about unicorns."

Mrs. Xia nods. "I believe I have a few that might interest you. Let me show you where they are."

I have spent so much time here that Mrs. Xia could probably just direct me to the titles or authors and I would be able to find the books from there. But I know from personal experience how much she enjoys helping students find special books, so I follow her to the back of the library.

She points to the middle row of shelves near the back door. "All the books about mythological creatures are in this section." She runs her hand across the spines of the books. "Let's see here— dragons, fairies, mermaids—ah, here we are. Unicorns." With a smile, Mrs. Xia hands me three books with unicorns on the covers.

"Mrs. Xia, we need your help," Bryden interrupts. He and Will B stand there looking very confused. "We can't find any books about pythons."

"Or cobras," Will B adds.

"Ah, snakes. Another subject I would rather see in a book," Mrs. Xia says with a smile in my direction.

I nod. I couldn't agree more.

Mrs. Xia glances at Bryden and Will B and then back at me. "I'll let you take a look at these for a few minutes."

I can tell already that none of these are exactly what I am looking for, but since I don't want to be rude, I thank her anyway. I am looking for a book about real unicorns, and these books are all about fairy-tale unicorns. Maybe I'll have to choose another subject after all.

I sigh and turn to slip the books back in their spot on the shelf. I help out a lot in the library, so I'm an expert at knowing how to reshelve a book. Two of the books go in perfectly, but the third one won't slide all the way back. It keeps stopping. I push again, but it won't budge. I am wasting time when I need to be finding a book. But I don't want to leave the book out of place or stuck on another shelf. That's one of my pet peeves—when library books are left in the wrong spots, so the next person who is looking for them can't find them. A library only works if every book is exactly where it is supposed to be. So I pull the book all the way out to try again.

And that's when I see it.

A tiny moss-green book is stuck in the back. It's turned sideways across the shelf behind the other books, so it might have been hidden here for years. There is no title on the front of the book, but a gold unicorn shape is stamped into the cover.

Suddenly, I no longer hear my friends talking at the table on the other side of the room. I don't hear Will P telling Mrs. Sablinsky some of his favorite facts about polar bears. I don't even hear the rustle of countless pages being turned.

The room has gone silent. I hear nothing at

all except my own breathing and the superfast beating of my heart. The unicorn on the cover is highlighted in a golden spotlight from the sun coming through the window behind me. Before I even touch the book, I know it's special. I can't say how I know this—only that I do.

(Sometimes a truly magical thing happens in a story that changes everything.)

I gently pull the book off the shelf. It's really small, only a little bit bigger than my hand. If I hadn't been putting the other books away, I never would have found it, which can only mean one thing.

It was meant to be.

I was meant to find this book today. I am meant to read it. Now I just have to find out why.

CHAPTER 4

And Introducing Lavender Lakewood

I sit down crisscross applesauce on the floor and open the little green book.

On the first page, it says, *"The Search for the Missing Unicorn by Lavender Lakewood."* Underneath the title are these words: "The Research and Notes of the Last True Unicorn Seeker, 1920."

In my heart, I hoped that something like this book existed, but to actually discover it hidden away in my own school library? It's a take-your-breath-away moment—the kind of moment you know you will remember forever. It's just that special.

I am no longer me. I am the last true unicorn seeker. I travel through a forest thick with trees, where sunlight peeks through the shade and leaves patterns on the ground. I wear my regular clothes with a special jacket that has lots of pockets to hold my journal and pen, flashlight, granola bar, and water. I must map my steps, for the forest is never-ending and looks the same at every turn. I see prints in the dirt. I follow them and discover that they are fox prints. I could say this is because of the shape and size of the print, but it's really because the fox is waiting for me. He decides to come along as my helper. I call him Buddy.

I start to turn to page one, but I hear Mrs. Sablinsky's voice. It appears her voice can be heard even when all other sounds have faded away and someone is having a special once-in-a-lifetime experience.

"You have ten minutes to get your choices approved and checked out."

I know I should stand up and get in line. But I have to peek at page one. I just have to. So I do it. I turn the page.

This is what I read:

My connection with unicorns began at the age of eight when I saw one in a dream. From that moment on, I knew it was my responsibility to study these beautiful creatures and to prove their existence to a world of nonbelievers.

I close the book very carefully, as if it might crumble in my hands. Then I hurry over to get approval from Mrs. Sablinsky.

Most of the class is in line at Mrs. Xia's desk,

checking out their books. A few of us are still getting approval. I am the last in line. Siri is right in front of me. She holds up a book about lions.

"What do you think?" she asks.

I grin. "I highly approve," I say in my fake British accent.

"My other choice was to get a book about whales. But I can draw a lion way better than I can draw a whale."

That's pretty smart. I didn't even think about the drawing part. I'm only OK at drawing unicorns, but I still won't change my mind. How could I after reading the first words of this magical book?

"What did you choose?" Siri wants to know.

I hold up the little book for her to see. Her eyes get really big, and she gives me a hug. "That's so perfect!"

It is perfect. We are the Unicorns after all. That's what I'm thinking as I show the book to my teacher. I expect her to say the same thing to me that she has said to every other student before me: "Approved."

Except that she doesn't.

She says this instead: "Ruby, this is a nonfiction book report. You need to choose a real subject."

If Will P hadn't just challenged me on the same topic, I might have accepted this and turned away sadly to choose a book about wolves or tigers. Truth: I'm not that great at drawing four-legged animals because the legs always turn out like upside-down Popsicles. (A wolf can't run on Popsicle legs.) But I have already practiced my argument, so I'm not discouraged by her disapproval. Instead, I smile and open the first page for her to see.

"Some people think unicorns aren't real because they don't exist anymore, but dinosaurs don't exist anymore either. Lavender Lakewood searched for clues about unicorns in the real world."

Mrs. Sablinsky purses her lips. *Don't let her*

sigh. *If she sighs, it's over*, I think. There is one more thing I can say to convince her, but it will only work if she has ever wanted to read a book as much as I want to read this book. It's worth a try.

"It was hidden behind the other books like a treasure. At the back of the bookshelf." I swallow and look right into her eyes. Dad says direct eye contact is very important when you want someone to hear what you have to say. "Have you ever read the first page of a book and known somehow in that moment that it was special? That it would change your life?"

Mrs. Sablinsky does the eyebrow thing where they rise so high they disappear underneath her hair. Uh-oh. This is not going to end well.

Then I do the only thing I can do, I push the book into her hands. "Maybe you could take a look at it."

She opens the cover and reads the first page.

Her lips press together into a thin line as she flips through the rest of the pages. I'm not sure if this is a good thing or not. I put a sugary-sweet expression on my face. I don't want to be too pushy or too whiny.

Finally, after what seems like forever but is probably less than a minute, she hands the book back to me. I notice that her lips are in two parts again and her eyebrows have come back to their usual places above her eyes. "It does appear to set forth Miss Lakewood's scientific research; therefore, I believe you are correct. The book falls into the nonfiction category."

My smile starts to stretch out from sweet to ecstatic, which also means going from a no-teeth smile to a full-teeth smile. Except that Mrs. Sablinsky isn't finished yet. "However, it is less than one hundred pages." My smile freezes right there with half-teeth showing, which might also be the same face I make when I am carsick. I might as well be carsick with the churning of my stomach at the word *however*. Most of the time, the words that follow *however* are not in my favor.

My teacher hands the book back to me, and I check the last page number—eighty-nine. I'm careful not to look at any of the words on the page. I don't want to accidentally read the ending and break one of my own book rules. I keep my eyes glued to the top of the page where the number is. I double-check it to be sure. It's definitely only eighty-nine pages.

Eleven pages short. Most people would give up and find something else right about now. I am not most people. I am an expert at coming up with a plan B. Even a plan C. And once or twice, I have even been known to go as far as a plan D. The key to making things happen is never giving up. That's what my grandpa tells me all the time. Plan B is out of my mouth before I even have time to think about what I am saying (this is one of my problems—speaking before thinking).

"What if I can find a second book by this same author? Could I read two books instead of one?"

Mrs. Sablinsky taps her fingers together and presses them against her mouth while she considers. Finally, she says, "I suppose so. Please bring the other book to school so I can approve it though."

I can barely contain my excitement. "I will." I hug the book tight and am about to head for the other line to check out when I remember something. "Thank you, Mrs. Sablinsky. I knew you would understand."

She gives me a really big smile and her eyebrows stay put. "I'm looking forward to reading your report."

Back in the classroom, Mrs. S moves right into a new social studies unit on the Revolutionary War. We take turns reading the chapter out loud. Then we have to answer discussion questions at the end.

"You can work with your neighbors if you like," she offers. Now that I am surrounded by my besties, this is wonderful news. We answer the questions really fast, and it's like a study group because I learn a lot and have fun at the same time.

"If you are finished, you can read quietly or choose a word search or a math puzzle from the box," Mrs. S tells us as she walks by.

Siri and Charlotte stand up to go to the back of the room for a word search. "You coming?" Charlotte asks.

I really like word searches, but I have a new book on my desk. "I can't wait to read my book" is my answer.

"Me too," Jessica adds. She holds up her book, *The Wild Mustang*. It has a photo of a herd of horses running in a meadow.

Daisy puts her pencil down. "I'll go."

Jessica opens her book and starts reading. I

am about to do the same when my seat neighbor asks me a question.

"She approved unicorns?" Will points to my book.

"My argument won her over. I guess I should thank you."

"No thanks necessary. I'm impressed." Will grins at me and then picks up his own book. He's reading about dinosaurs after all.

I shrug, even though it's nice to receive a compliment. My mom would probably tell me to say thank you, so I do. "Thanks. But you haven't heard all of it yet. I'm eleven pages short of one hundred, so I have to read a second book too."

Will's eyes get super-big behind his glasses. "Two books in one report. That's almost like doing two book reports. I hope it's worth it."

It will be. I just know it.

Now it's time for less talking and more reading, I think. Lavender Lakewood is waiting.

I start where I left off:

From that moment on, I knew it was my responsibility to study these beautiful creatures and to prove their existence to a world of non-believers. So I began compiling evidence. The first written record of unicorns comes from the writing of Ctesias, a Greek historian from the fourth century BC. He identified a powerful beast with a white body, a crimson head, blue eyes, and a single horn on its head. The Old Testament mentions unicorns multiple times. In medieval times, unicorns were often depicted in writing and in artwork such as tapestries and paintings. All over the world, there are references to an animal that is similar to a horse or a goat with a single horn on its head. In China, this animal is called a qilin. The horn itself was valued because it could cure many kinds of illnesses and protect against poisons. My theory is that these animals were hunted to near extinction for their horns. I say "near extinction" because

I believe there may be unicorns left in the world.
Someone only needs to find them.

I am in a bookstore, signing my first book called
Unicorns For Real. People from all over have come to
meet me because I have seen a unicorn with my own eyes.
They are lined up all the way out the door and down the
street. Even Mrs. Sablinsky and Mrs. Xia are here, which is
amazing. Will B and Bryden are also here, which is not so
amazing. My family is really proud of me. I have proven the
existence of the unicorn.

Suddenly, the lunch bell rings, startling me. I'm in Room 15, not at my first book signing.

"Ruby? Are you sleeping with your eyes open?" Siri is waving her hand in front of my eyes.

I blink.

"Just thinking," I answer before I hurry to get my lunch from my backpack. Then the Unicorns walk together to the lunch tables.

Our mission for today is to find a new place to eat.

"I hope we can find a table far away from flying food," Jessica shares.

I grin at her. "Me too."

Only finding a new place to sit isn't as easy as it sounds. Because there are only a few empty spots here and there, but not enough room at any of the tables for all five of us.

We walk around the lunch area once. Twice. We are about to circle a third time when the aide stops us.

"Girls, please take a seat," she says with a frown. Causing trouble at lunch can result in the dreaded trash pickup assignment. Nothing is worse than picking up other people's leftover food and wrappers (except maybe having an unknown gooey object stuck in your hair).

We have to make a decision—and fast. Our time is running out.

"The only way we can move is if we split up," Charlotte says softly.

"And that is not an option," Siri finishes.

Daisy shrugs. "Well, I'm hungry." Then she breaks from the group and heads for our usual table.

I sigh as the rest of us follow her.

I sit between Siri and Charlotte. Jessica and Daisy sit on the other side. Will P and his food-fight friends are at the far end of the table, but at least they aren't throwing food. Not yet, anyway. Mom has made me my usual today. I decide to eat the turkey sandwich now and leave the apple and pretzels for after.

"We didn't get to choose a book for next week," I say as I sip from my water bottle. "Any ideas?"

"If we have to read a book for class, I might not have time to read one for book club too," Daisy tells me.

"Maybe we can choose one, but give ourselves more time to finish," Charlotte suggests.

"That's a good idea," I agree.

Jessica has a different idea. "Maybe we could talk about our book report books instead."

I think about this. It might be fun to share our different subjects.

I am sitting at the lunch tables with the Unicorn Book Club,
only instead of just talking about the books we are reading,
we each have our subjects with us. Siri is sitting next to a
lion wearing a bow tie, Jessica has a mustang in hair ribbons
by her side, Daisy is paired with a wolf in sneakers, Charlotte
is matched with a gorilla in a tutu, and I have invited a
unicorn in a crown. All of the animal guests are holding the
books about them. They are happy to talk about themselves
until the food fight starts at the other end of the table.

"Book club is about reading a book together
as a group." Siri's eyes look sad again. I'm pretty
sure she's going to cry. Crying over book club

has happened to me once (I even broke the Ruby Starr No Crying at School Rule). But it's never happened to Siri before.

Of all the Unicorns, Jessica and I are the ones who love reading the most. There was a time when Siri was even part of a vote to change the book club to a drama club. So Siri talking about how important it is to read a book together is just another thing that seems different. I know Gram said I needed to be patient and wait for Siri to talk to me, but patience is not my best skill. I take a big breath and try to figure out what to do. But before I can come up with any great ideas, Charlotte comes up with her own great idea.

"Let's vote," she suggests. "Everyone who wants to talk about our book report books, raise your hand."

I raise my hand. So does Jessica. Then Daisy raises her hand, too. Now all of us except Charlotte and Siri have our hands in the air. Siri just looks down at her water bottle. She twists the cap back and forth. The vote is three to two.

"It looks like we're sharing book report reads," I announce.

"You don't understand," Siri begins, but then stops talking. Her eyes are super-shiny, and her bottom lip is pulled tight in a straight line like if she lets it loose, it will say things she doesn't want to say.

"It's just for next week," I tell her. "After that, we'll be done with our book reports and we can read a new book together."

"It will be too late," Siri blurts out.

"Too late for what?" Jessica asks.

But Siri just shakes her head. "Forget it."

When someone says to forget something, they are usually saying that they won't forget it. It's like a secret way of saying that they will be remembering. So you have to remember too. Only it's kind of a problem when you have no idea what it is you're supposed to be remembering.

CHAPTER 5

The Un-Wednesday Wednesday

Mom has her book club meetings on Wednesday nights. Mom's book club was the inspiration for my book club, so I am kind of an honorary member. Tonight, though, there is no meeting.

"With the holidays coming, everyone was so busy. Only a few of us would have been able to make it, and we thought it was better to cancel the book club for the rest of the month," Mom explains in the car on the way home from school.

"We're still getting pizza though, right?" I love our regular order from Charlie's Pizza. Knowing that the three pizzas will arrive at exactly six o'clock is one of those things that's always the same—exactly the way I like it.

"We're only getting two pizzas tonight, but yes, there will be pizza." Mom is wearing her non-office clothes today. She's in a blue-and-white floral shirt, jeans, and brown boots. Also, her hair is loose and curly just like mine, but hers behaves better. "Now, tell me all about your day."

I take a big breath and begin. I have a lot to tell, and Mom has time to listen. By the time we get to Connor's school, Mom knows all about my unicorn book. "It's truly inspiring to hear about a young woman in the early 1900s believing in her own theories and setting out to prove them true. I think my book club would like to read this book of yours."

I have never suggested a book to Mom's group, mostly because I wouldn't know what they like to read, but also because it's a bit on the intimidating side. I mean, they're my mom's friends. To have Mom tell me that a book I've

chosen is something her group would be interested in reading...well, let's just say it makes me
very proud. And happy.

My brothers take charge of the conversation the
minute they get into the car. First, we pick up
Connor, who tells my mom about all the good
grades he received today. (Can you guess what
letter is all over his report cards? I'll give you one
hint: it's the first in the alphabet.) Then we pick
up Sam at his school. He talks about the class he
has to take before getting his driver's permit.

"I can't wait until you can drive me to a movie
and the bookstore," I tell him. Sam is riding in the
front seat. Connor and I are in the back. Riding
in the front seat is a daily discussion between my
brothers. Actually, calling it a "discussion" is a
nice way of putting it.

"I can't wait until the front seat is mine,"

Connor adds with a grin at me. He looks just like Dad when he smiles.

"I'll take you to the bookstore and the library every week," Sam promises. He hands a peanut butter granola bar over the seat to me. Then he hands one to Connor.

"Not so fast," Mom cuts in. "You won't be driving anyone but yourself for the first year." Then she says to Connor, "And you will need to share the front seat with Ruby in the next couple of years."

He groans as though he's not too happy about this news, but he winks at me to let me know he's just teasing.

"There's no book club tonight," I tell my brothers.

"Are we still having Charlie's?" Sam asks.

"Is that all my family cares about?" Mom is joking. We can tell since she is laughing.

"Yes!" my brothers and I call out at the same

time. And then everyone starts laughing. It isn't true, of course, but sometimes it feels good just to laugh, even if something is only a little bit funny. You laugh just because you want to.

The pizzas are on the kitchen counter, smelling delicious, and I'm helping Mom set the table. Abe is underneath the table, getting ready for dinnertime. Suddenly, he lets out a cry and dashes to the door, making a big commotion and knocking into Mom with his big, floppy paws. I always know someone from my family is about to walk in when Abe runs to the door like that. The amazing thing is that he knows before a car has even pulled into the garage, because we can all hear that. Maybe Abe is a one-of-a-kind dog-seer who can predict the future.

I imagine Abe sitting in the kitchen, wagging his tail across the floor as he watches me at the kitchen counter. Abe's thoughts appear in bubbles over his head. First, he sees a squirrel he wants to chase later. Then he sees himself sleeping on my bed. And last, he sees the bowl of kibble I am about to set down in front of him. I set the bowl down just as he predicted. Abe smiles to himself, proud of his talent and happy with his dinner.

Dad walks through the door, just as Abe told us he would.

"*Bonsoir,*" he says, greeting us with a French *good evening*. Dad isn't really French. He's learning the language to enrich himself. Dad says it's important to always keep learning. Next, he wants to learn to play the cello.

"*Bonsoir, mon père,*" I reply with a little of my own French. I know a few words from different languages. I think every writer should be able to sprinkle foreign languages into their work here and there.

I run over and hug my dad. He's a super-great hugger, especially when he picks me up off the ground. I know I'm ten, but even a ten-year-old likes to be picked up once in a while. "How was your day?" he asks me.

"Really exciting. I can't wait to tell you all about it." He sets me back on the ground, and I hurry to put a napkin by each of the five place settings.

"We are eating our pizzas together at the table tonight," Mom says as he kisses her hello. Sam and Connor are just coming into the kitchen at that moment. Both of them groan.

Mom pretends not to know why they are groaning, even though we all know what they mean. They want to eat pizza in front of the television.

After that, we all sit down. Mom has put all the pizza slices on plates, so it looks much fancier than in the cardboard boxes. The pizza is gooey and cheesy and super-yummy.

Everyone goes around the table sharing news from their day. I like the way my family really talks to each other. It doesn't seem like a Wednesday though, because usually Mom would be in the living room having her book club meeting, and I would be in there with her, listening. It's like a Wednesday that isn't really a Wednesday but is more like a Tuesday or a Thursday. Or even a Monday.

"I have an announcement," Connor says, borrowing one of my signature phrases—I don't mind sharing though. "My teacher really liked my essay about the praying mantis, so he submitted it to the school newspaper. It should be in by next week."

Everyone talks at once. See if you can guess who is saying what:

"*Bon travail.*"

"That is most excellent news" (said with a British accent).

"Congrats!"

"I am so proud of you."

"Arf, arf."

Then Sam has his own announcement. "I've been thinking about this a lot." He looks to me for encouragement. I already know what he is going to say because I helped him practice last night. "There are a lot of opportunities for chefs on television, and I want to start my own baking show."

"What a wonderful idea!" Mom is the first one to speak.

One glance at Dad tells me that he is thinking this over and isn't ready to say anything yet. Connor's mouth is filled with pizza. I have already told my brother that I think it's a better-than-best idea, and that I will film him (if he wants), and help him prepare his ingredients. I am better at baking than I used to be. I make much less of a mess since the cupcake fiasco (which turned out to be the opposite of a fiasco, but that's a whole other story).

Connor finishes his bite. "Let me know how I can help."

Finally, Dad weighs in. He clears his throat, which is what he usually does before he tells you something he thinks you probably don't want to hear. Uh-oh.

"I spend my life reporting on people who start businesses or charities or help the community because they follow a dream. All it takes is a spark of an idea and commitment to make it happen. I know you have more than that because you have talent."

OK, maybe this is going to go better than I thought. So far, it's super-positive.

I shoot a smile toward my brother. He looks nervous.

"I applaud your determination and your creativity." Dad clears his throat again. I am guessing the part Sam doesn't want to hear is coming now. "I just want to make sure you don't get discouraged and give up on your dream. Sometimes it takes a while to grow an audience."

Sam shakes his head. "I'm not worried about an audience. I just want to get experience explaining what I am cooking."

Dad smiles then. "In that case, you have my full support."

Just like that, everything is easy-peasy

lemon-squeezy again. It seems like the perfect time to tell everyone about my book discovery and the world of unicorn expeditions.

"There's only one problem though," I sigh. "The book is shorter than it's supposed to be, but I really wanted to read it. So I offered to read a second book to make up for it."

Mom pats me on the shoulder. "That was a very creative solution."

"I'm impressed," Connor says with his mouth full of pizza. This is super-gross when someone at school, for example Will B, speaks with his mouth full of salami. But it's different with my brother. It's still gross. Just not gross-gross.

I shrug. "I thought it was a great idea at the time, but now I'm not so sure. What if Lavender Lakewood didn't write any other books?"

Dad grins. "There's only one way to find out." He offers me another slice of pizza. "Did I ever tell you that I am an expert at researching?" I smile, because of course Dad is good at researching. He writes news stories for the local morning news. "I'll help you right after dinner," he promises.

Dad is true to his word, because while Mom and Connor clean up the kitchen, Dad and I head for the computer in the den. Dad has me sit in front of the computer while he takes the chair to the side. "I'm just here as a helper" is his reasoning.

"Start with searching for 'author Lavender Lakewood,'" Dad suggests.

I type "author" and her name into the search engine. A lot of entries pop up. One of them is a whole site devoted to Lavender. It's called *Lavender Lakewood—The Official Site.*

"I always start with an official site first, if there is one." Dad leans close. "I think of research as a treasure hunt. I'm searching through countless records to find the truth. Sometimes it takes patience, and sometimes it takes luck. But there is always treasure to be found."

I never thought of it that way before. Suddenly, looking for information about Lavender Lakewood is a whole lot more fun than it was a minute ago.

The website has a photo of her on the main page. It's one of those brownish, old-fashioned photos. Her dark hair is short and wavy, and she's wearing a white, buttoned shirt with a dark jacket over it. Even though she is looking right at the camera, she isn't smiling.

"She looks so sad in her picture," I say softly. Maybe searching for unicorns was a disappointing job for her.

"In those days, people didn't smile into the camera like we do now," Dad explains. "I wouldn't read too much into it."

Below her name is a description of her work and her book *The Search for the Missing Unicorn.*

Dad points to the computer screen. "Here, there is a mention of another published work."

I follow Dad's point to the words on the screen. The site says:

A second volume containing Miss Lakewood's additional field notes was published in 1923, three years after her original work. Miss Lakewood found a unicorn in her search, and yet she declined to reveal its location for fear that the animal would be captured. Instead, she left it free where she found it in the hope that, with this act, the unicorn would never completely disappear.

I jump out of the chair and turn to face my dad. "She found a unicorn! We have to get this book right away." All I can think are the clues in this book. Maybe I can go and find the unicorn too.

Dad hugs me. "I love your enthusiasm. Let's do a library search." I sit down again, and Dad shows me how to bring up our town's library website. Then I click on the box for "Search by

Author Name." I put in Lavender Lakewood. And guess what—it's there!

"Click on the tab to reserve the book." Dad wasn't kidding when he said he was an expert at researching. "That way it will be there when you go to pick it up."

"I'll ask Gram to take me tomorrow after school." I will be counting down the minutes until tomorrow afternoon.

I read a little of my book before bed. I learn more about Lavender's search for unicorns. When I fall asleep, the stories mash up so they become one, except now I am the person on the adventure.

The moon shines through the dark night, lighting a path for
me. I am not in the forest but inside a closed museum. The
map is in my hand, and Buddy the fox is by my side. I am
searching for the unicorn. I look behind the sculptures and
underneath the cases of pottery. Then I think to look at the
paintings. One by one, I check them until I find one with a
white unicorn nearly hidden in a forest of golden leaves. The
unicorn suddenly disappears behind the trees. I step through
the painting to follow him.

CHAPTER 6

A Roller-Coaster Day

Thursday morning, I hurry up the stairs to line up in front of Room 15. I am so focused on the clues to find a missing unicorn that I have completely forgotten about Siri and the vote yesterday. I remember the minute I reach the top of the stairs, because Siri looks like she might cry again. I ask her if she's OK, but she just shrugs and acts like nothing is wrong.

The bell rings, and Mrs. Sablinsky takes us into class. Siri is right in front of me, and we usually hang our backpacks side by side on the rack inside the room. Only today, she moves over and hangs hers at the end, next to Will B's backpack. Will B!

Mrs. Sablinsky rings her little bell, signaling the class to be quiet and listen. She begins to take roll. Since my name is near the end of the alphabet, I don't have to pay attention just yet.

I slump down in my seat and lean my head on my arm.

Siri is looking at the teacher with laser vision, as though if she looks away, she will suddenly be transported to another galaxy. Everyone can tell when someone is looking at them, even if that someone is looking at them from the side. That's how I know Siri can tell I am looking at her, even if she doesn't want me to know she knows. And that makes it even worse.

This is how I know that:

> something
>
>   is
>
>   very
>
>   wrong

(or wronger, if that
were a word, which
I am pretty sure
it's not).

I am so focused on Siri that I don't notice Mrs. Sablinsky calling me until Will waves his hand in front of my eyes. "Ruby, it's your name."

"Here," I call out immediately. "Thanks for the quick save," I whisper to Will.

"No problem," he whispers back.

I look Siri's way again. She still has her eyes latched on to the teacher. I wonder what would happen if I called her name. Would she look at me, or would she ignore me? I decide to give it a try.

"Siri," I whisper. "Siri."

Nothing.

"Hello there," I try again.

Still nothing.

OK, now this is getting embarrassing. It

might have even crossed the border of embarrassing and moved into humiliating territory.

Fine. If she doesn't want to talk to me, then I won't talk to her either. This is called the Shun. We have been here before, and it requires a special warning: *Be prepared. The Shun can be extremely upsetting to witness.* The Shun is when someone who usually wouldn't ignore you pretends you don't exist. It's awfully miserable to receive the Shun, but it's even worse to give someone the Shun because you always end up regretting it.

I know I will regret it, but I can't let myself be shunned without shunning in return. (This is one of those times when I should have learned from my lowercase *m* mistakes, but I haven't really. Or I haven't learned enough, anyway.) That's why I stop looking at Siri or calling her name. From this moment on, we will be invisible to each other.

While all of this drama is going on in my

personal life, my teacher is trying to start class. After Bryden walks in late, and she has to wake up Jason twice, she makes an announcement.

"I have some big news for Room 15. In connection with your book reports and research on the natural world, we will be having a field trip next Thursday."

Field trips aren't really that exciting at my school, since most of the time we stay here and the activity comes to us. So the field trips aren't really trips, but assemblies that are called "field trips," which is completely misleading if you ask me.

Plus, I haven't had the greatest time at them. The last field trip that wasn't really a field trip involved taking off shoes and walking on a giant map. The map part would have been fun if it hadn't been for my mismatched socks, which were on display for the entire fifth grade to see. (And the fact that my partner was giving me the Shun at the time.)

Then Mrs. S says something that completely and totally surprises me:

"We will be going to the Natural History Museum."

This isn't just big news. This is the biggest news in the history of fifth grade. A real field trip! The whole class starts cheering, and for a split second, I completely forget about Siri and the Shun because I am clapping and hollering along with the rest of Room 15 about this awesome news.

"I am handing out permission slips that you must have signed by your parent or guardian and returned by next Monday. We will be leaving on the bus right after roll call and not returning until after lunch, so you will need to bring a sack lunch for yourself that day."

I try not to notice that Siri has turned around to ask Charlotte to sit with her on the bus. Everyone knows that best friends sit together on bus rides. It's one of those things that is reserved for best friends, like sleepovers and special handshakes. Of course, Daisy and Jessica will sit together. So that leaves me... partnerless.

Also known as the worst possible situation to be in. This day has gone from amazing to awful to amazing to awful like a giant roller coaster zooming up and down. The last time our family went to an amusement park, I tried the roller coaster with Connor. One minute, I had my hands in the air, woo-hoo-ing. And the next minute, I was gripping my brother's arm and begging to get off the ride. I check the clock. This roller coaster of a day has happened in less than fifteen minutes.

Suddenly, I am not looking forward to the field trip anymore. I'm not even looking forward to reading more of Lavender Lakewood's book. I just want to go home.

The day gets worse from there. Mrs. Sablinsky decides to give us a pop quiz on the metric system. After the test, I take a peek at the word search box. Last time I looked in here, I had done all of the searches. But it looks like she's added some new ones. I choose a star in honor of my last name.

```
                    T
                    G
                  Z I S
                  W Y P
                  J S O
                C M V T G
                S A G L N
                M T Z I Z
              I X I X G W E
              N F N S H S V
              H D E O T V J
  S Q K L N F K R R M N V Y E W P R E M I E R E D M F M S R
    E X R A F E C U X S P E C T A C U L A R G C H B R Z A
      T Z U L P E R F O R M A N C E M L V U M H W S
      Q F D X A P P L A U S E H C S F V A A T U
        J K I M I D L H C X M W V B K R K G Q
          E E H T H E A T R I C A L F C
          Z N H U O P T P T G J Z U
            E C R R U B O C D R M
            G R E I N Y M O Q L Y
            W Y K U D Q V R D V W
          K Y D M T Q I K F Z X M Y
          N E N T E R T A I N V I S
          B S Z B E W   B L Y F U L
        F D L O T C         L O B A I C
        O S D H J           F G X Y O
        C D K               U W I
      K D L                   E Z F
      C D                     Q C
      W                         Q
```

spotlight	audience	spectacular
entertain	performance	theatrical
dialogue	premiere	
applause	matinee	

I find all of the words except for one: *spotlight*. I look and look at the star, but I just don't see it. Dad says sometimes if you can't find the answer to a problem, you need to look at it from a different perspective. I turn the star sideways, but I still can't find the missing word.

I don't have more time anyway, because Mrs. S has another announcement for us. But this time, it isn't going to make me or anyone else in class cheer.

"I have to go to a district meeting, and there is a sub coming for the rest of the day." Chatter fills the room as everyone talks about having a sub for the rest of the day. It could be someone fantastic like Mrs. Xia...

The door creaks open as though in slow motion. *Creeeeeeeeeeeeeeeeeeeeaaaaaaak!*

Or it could be this really awful substitute teacher we had once, named—

"Mrs. Cheer, there you are," Mrs. S says to the unfriendliest sub ever in the history of subs.

And there she is. She's already wearing her pretend I'm-happy-to-be-here smile, but I know from past experience that she is anything but happy to sub this class. Mrs. Cheer is most definitely not cheery.

Mrs. Sablinsky gives us lots of social studies questions to be followed by spelling words and sentences. Everyone in class works without even a giggle. Maybe that's because Mrs. Cheer will write down the name of any student who is not behaving on the board. Or maybe it's because whatever we don't finish in class will be homework.

I'm so busy with the assignments that I actually forget about Siri and the Shun—until the bell rings for lunch. Because it all comes zooming back into my mind when I see Siri rush out the door next to Charlotte without even waiting for me.

I join Jessica and Daisy for the walk down the stairs and to the lunch tables. I try not to think about why Siri is mad at me. I also try not to think about an entire afternoon with Mrs. Cheer.

"I can't believe how much work Mrs. Sablinsky left for us today," Daisy complains. I pull off my sweatshirt and tie it around my waist. It is as warm as a summer day today even though it's December.

"She probably wants to keep us busy so we don't cause any trouble for Mrs. Cheer." Jessica would make a good teacher when she grows up—she seems to understand the way teachers think.

This is one of those times when I would rather tag along than talk. When we get to the lunch tables, I take the seat on the end of the bench, next to Daisy. Siri and Charlotte are on the other side of the table. Charlotte gives me a smile with a shrug. I think it's a message without words to tell me that she's sorry for leaving me out. Siri is still not looking at me. But I'm not looking at her either (well, actually I *am* looking at her, or I wouldn't know that she isn't looking at me).

Everyone else is eating their lunches and chatting away. It's like they don't even notice that two best friends are not speaking. I can't possibly eat at a time like this, so I don't bother to open my lunch to see what Mom sent for me today. I just sip from my water bottle and pretend to listen to everyone talk about the field trip. A field trip where we actually leave school is definitely something to celebrate, unless you know that you are already going to be partnerless. In which case, you will be matched up with someone by your teacher. This means that another student who is partnerless will become your partner. I consider the options for this scenario—Jason, who sleeps through class almost every day, or Will B, who likes to eat random objects that are not actually food, are the two students who are most likely to be partnerless.

Maybe I can come up with an illness that will keep me out of school next Thursday. Anything would be better than facing a day with a partner chosen by my teacher because I can't get one on my own.

"Fairy-tale mash-up at lunch today?" Charlotte asks. On Thursdays, we play a drama game. Today is supposed to be a fairy-tale mash-up, where each of us chooses a main character from a fairy tale to represent.

"Count me in," I answer.

When the aide blows her whistle, I don't have to pack up my lunch bag because I have never even opened it. That makes me the first one standing up.

"I'm going to the swings," Siri says before taking off by herself.

Charlotte watches her walk away and then looks back to me. Daisy and Jessica are looking back and forth too. Finally, everyone is noticing the something that is very wrong. No one says anything about it, which is a good thing because even though Siri isn't talking to me, I don't want to talk about her. That would make the something wrong even worse. (Trust me, I know this from past experience. This is one thing I *have* learned from my lowercase *m* mistakes.)

"What do you want to do?" I ask Jessica.

Jessica shrugs. "Drama Thursdays. That's what we always do."

It's not so much fun to act out a play when one of the cast members is missing. Even though we all take a part (I am Red Riding Hood), there's tension in the air like a thundercloud hovering over us. Any minute, we expect to get zapped with lightning. We just don't know when.

I am Little Red Riding Hood heading through the forest to bring my grandmother a jar of pickles on a cloudy day. A thundercloud bursts overhead, and jagged streaks of lightning begin to crack the sky into pieces. As the sky falls down around me, I dash for cover to the nearest shelter I see, which is a house made of bricks. This used to be the house of the Three Little Pigs, but they moved to London, so now a wolf lives here. The wolf is actually friendly and offers me the starring role in his new musical about the power of friendship. He's an excellent tap dancer, and he makes a delicious apple pie.

CHAPTER 7

The Most Awful Friday: Part 1

The end of the day is spent running around the schoolyard for PE, followed by games of basketball. Mrs. Cheer actually looks sort of happy about this activity. I'm guessing this is because she can sit on the lunch benches and read a book while we exercise. I can't really blame her though. I would rather be reading than running. I'd rather be doing anything than running, even dividing fractions.

I usually run with Siri. But today everything is different. I end up running by myself. Running alone is B-O-R-I-N-G! We already know how I feel about change, so this is not good for me—not good at all.

(Heroes in books sometimes have to face challenges all on their own because no one else will stand by them. It happens.)

By the time the bell rings and I can hurry out to the front of school to meet Gram, I am exhausted. Who knew the Shun could be so tiring?

"Hi, pumpkin," Gram says, greeting me with a hug. "How was your day?"

If I start telling her the whole story here, I might break the Ruby Starr No Crying at School Rule. That would make this day the official worst day ever in the history of days. So instead of going into all the details, I just say this: "Good and bad. Could you take me to the library to pick up a book? It would make the bad part a whole lot better."

Gram is the best when it comes to worser-than-worse days. She sweeps my backpack over her shoulder and puts her arm around me. "Let's make this day a whole lot better then."

As she drives Grambus to the library, I tell her my good news about the field trip. This I can talk about without getting upset.

"The Natural History Museum is filled with wonderful exhibits." I can see her smile in the rearview mirror but not the rest of her face. "I can't wait to hear all about it."

My stomach grumbles just then, and it's loud enough for Gram to hear. "I think there's a bear caught inside your stomach," she says.

Here's my top list of most embarrassing things to happen to you at school:

1. Vomiting (this happened to Daisy once, and after she threw up on her desk, everyone ran out of the room screaming)
2. Stomach gurgles
3. Having something green or black stuck in your teeth

Lucky for me my stomach waited to do its gurgling until *after school.*

"I didn't really eat my lunch," I explain to Gram. I didn't eat my lunch at all on account of the person who is supposed to be my best friend since kindergarten is giving me the Shun because I voted against her in book club. But I don't add all that. I'm not ready to talk about it yet. And anyway, we will be at the library in a few minutes and there is barely enough time to go in and get my unicorn book. I don't want to start talking about something that takes way more time than it takes to eat a granola bar to explain.

But I do have enough time to eat a granola bar. And lucky for me, Mom has packed one in my lunch today. I hurry to bite into it. Yum. It has raisins. The little surprise of biting into a granola bar and finding a raisin boosts my energy and gives me a little spring in my step. I hurry to the children's section of the library.

Gram is right beside me. She's a sporty grandma, so she can keep up with a ten-year-old who has a springy step.

My favorite librarian, Miss Mary, is here today. She isn't wearing her usual style of a colorful cardigan and flowered skirt. Instead, she is dressed up as Dorothy! For book people like me, when someone says *Dorothy*, we automatically know the person is referring to the one and only Dorothy from *The Wonderful Wizard of Oz*. Miss Mary is wearing a blue-and-white-checked apron dress with a white, puffy-sleeved shirt underneath. Her curly brown hair is in two braids tied with blue ribbons, she has a basket over her arm, and on her feet are silver, sparkly slippers. (Fun factoid: the ruby slippers Dorothy wears in the movie were a change from the silver ones in the book because the red looked better on film. I'm a movie trivia whiz!)

"Hi, Miss Mary. I love your outfit!" I smile

as I peek inside the basket. There's an actual dog stuffed animal in there.

"Hi, Ruby. You got here at the perfect time. I just returned from Oz." She clicks her silver heels together. "We're celebrating children's literature today by dressing up as our favorite characters."

That's when I notice that other librarians are wearing costumes too. I see a knight, a genie, a pioneer, and the Queen of Hearts all walking around the library.

"What a wonderful idea," Gram says with a smile.

"I wish we could dress up every day," Miss Mary adds. "I had a hard time choosing."

I nod and grin. "I know what you mean. I can think of at least ten characters I could be." I consider listing them for Miss Mary, but I know time is ticking away, and I need to get my book checked out. That's why I cut the chitchat and get to business. "My dad and I reserved a book for checkout today. It's by Lavender Lakewood."

"Ah, searching for unicorns today?" I'm not surprised that Miss Mary has read the book. She knows absolutely everything about children's literature. There isn't a title that she hasn't already read.

Miss Mary goes to the front desk. Gram and I don't sit down like we usually do because this will be a short visit. The book is already reserved, and I know it's here.

She returns speedy quick with a small book in her hand. This one is raspberry colored, but it has the same gold unicorn on the front. My skin starts to tingle the minute I see it. When she places it in my hands, a shiver runs down my neck. It's not a scary kind of shiver, like when you read a spooky part of a story—it's more like a one-of-a-kind moment shiver.

I open to the first page.

Here is what it says:

Volume II of the Field Notes of the Last True Unicorn Seeker, 1923 by Lavender Lakewood.

I close the book and hug it tight. Sometimes when a book is even better than you dreamed it would be, your heart is so filled with joy that you might just float up into the sky like a rainbow bubble. That's how it is for me in this exact moment—like nothing could possibly get any better than this.

But guess what. It does.

(Sometimes in a story, an important piece of information comes from an unexpected person and this piece of information takes the story in a completely new direction.)

Miss Mary says something that makes me totally speechless.

"Did you know that there's an exhibit about Lavender Lakewood at the Natural History Museum right now?"

I think my mouth is hanging open because she gives me a kind of funny look. But there's more.

"Some say there is a hidden message in her work, but no one has ever been able to decode it. Historians believe the message is a map to the location of the unicorn. I think you can learn anything from books, which is why I'm sure the secret is there somewhere."

A secret map? Written in code? I can't believe my ears.

My mouth opens even wider. I must look very odd or like I am about to cough. I find my words after what must be a few very awkward seconds for Gram and Miss Mary, but for me are a spinning, glittery top of ideas and thoughts. I try to explain them all in one single sentence. "I am going to the Natural History Museum next week!"

Miss Mary jumps right into the air at that information. Her braids bob up and down and the stuffed dog flies up out of the basket on her arm. "Oh, how exciting! What a wonderful coincidence."

In my world, there is no such thing as a coincidence. Everything happens for a reason.

I am back in the forest, only now I am dressed as Dorothy but with sneakers instead of heels. Sneakers are way more practical footwear for exploring in a forest. Buddy the fox sits in the basket on my arm. I hold a map in my hand that can only be deciphered with the notes in the field guide. Buddy and I sit down by a lake to decode the message. When the moon and stars reflect off the water, I click my silver sneakers, and a unicorn appears. He touches his horn to the page in my notebook, and the code words light up to form a map. When I look up from the map, the unicorn has disappeared.

"We better get this checked out now," Gram gently reminds me.

"Thank you for your help, Miss Dorothy," I use her character name instead of her real one. When book people are dressed up as characters, we like to really *be* the characters.

"Come back to Oz anytime," she answers with a wink. "I look forward to hearing all about the unicorn exhibit."

I wave as we head to the main counter to check out the book. I can't wait to start reading.

The next morning, I am the first person in line for class. Actually, I am the only person in line for class. It's raining today, so I am using my white and silver umbrella with wings like Pegasus. My plan is to ask Mrs. Sablinsky about the Lavender Lakewood exhibit before roll call. But sometimes plans don't go exactly as planned.

Because I have completely forgotten that this is Friday.

Which explains why no one else is in line. On Fridays, the entire school meets in the auditorium where we have our weekly assemblies. I can't believe I didn't remember this. I leave my backpack near the classroom door, where it is underneath the edge of the roof, so it won't get wet. And then I slosh through the puddles and back down the stairs.

Now, instead of being early, I am probably going to be late. I run-walk to make it on time, slip through the door, and put down my umbrella. Mom says when someone uses an umbrella, it's important to have umbrella courtesy. That means closing your umbrella inside and holding the pointy end down, so you don't accidentally poke someone.

I guess Will B never learned umbrella courtesy because, instead of holding his closed umbrella with the pointy end down, he is waving it in front of him like a sword. Bryden is doing the exact same thing. Wait a minute, they aren't just waving the umbrellas like swords—they are fighting with the umbrellas. The two of them clang back and forth and trample all the backpacks on the floor. Then Bryden trips and tumbles over. Will B presses the umbrella against his chest.

Things are about to get dangerous when Principal Snyder lifts the umbrella right out of Will B's hand. "I will be keeping this until the end of the day." He helps Bryden up from the ground. Then he opens his hand. "I'll take care of yours as well." Bryden turns over his umbrella to the principal. "Very well. Now, please find your seats."

Principal Snyder steps back to give me room to pass by and greets me as though nothing just happened. "Good morning, Ruby." I guess a principal would be used to things like umbrella-sword fights.

"Good morning." I walk around the backpacks

on the floor, which is a maze of leopard and polka dots and even faux fur. I'm really careful not to step on any of them. No one likes a giant, dirty rain boot print on their pink-and-white-striped roller backpack.

I look at the auditorium, and my stomach drops like there's a huge rose quartz crystal in there instead of a strawberry smoothie and scrambled egg. Because Siri didn't save me a seat. She always saves me a seat (or I save her a seat if I get here first). I can tell that the entire Room 15 row is full. The only seat left is on the end of the row next to Mrs. Sablinsky. A little prick touches the back of my right eyeball. It's not an actual tear but the beginning of one. I blink it away really fast and paste a smile on my face that isn't my real smile, but is the "everything is fine even though it's not" smile I wear when absolutely necessary. Then I take the seat next to my teacher.

The bad part of this situation is that I am

not sitting with my friends, so the things that are usually fun about the assembly—like cheering for the upcoming winter break in two weeks, or crossing fingers when Principal Snyder announces which class has won the spirit trophy this week— aren't really fun at all. It's pretty sad when you are looking forward to your spelling test.

The good part of this situation is that when there is a break in the assembly, I can ask Mrs. S the question I hoped to ask before roll call. Sometimes when you get lemons, you have to make lemonade—that's what I always say.

I smile at my teacher and say this: "I found a second book by my author. I brought it today so you could approve it."

Mrs. Sablinsky must have had her coffee this morning because she returns my smile and seems happy for me. "That's terrific. Why don't you show it to me after the spelling test?"

Since she's in a happy mood, I say the thing

I have been planning to say since yesterday afternoon. "Guess what I just found out." I don't wait for her to guess. "There is an exhibit about my book at the Natural History Museum!"

Mrs. Sablinsky smiles even bigger. "It really is special, isn't it?" She is referring to what I said when I found the first book in the library. But she hasn't answered my question yet.

Then I realize that I haven't actually asked her the question. The super-important-change-everything question. So I do.

"Can we see the exhibit when we are at the museum next week? I looked it up last night, and it will only be there for another few days. Then it's moving to a museum in New York." New York is across the country. This is a really strong argument for seeing the exhibit while it's in California. It may be my only possible chance.

I expect Mrs. S to smile again and nod. She doesn't. I watch as her smile literally turns upside down. My smile shrinks at the same time. "I'm sorry, Ruby. Our day is already planned out. We are seeing the mammal hall and the insects, followed by the dinosaur exhibit. I do have a surprise though."

My eyebrows raise a little at that—not all the way until they disappear underneath my hair, but a little higher than usual.

She shakes her head. "It's not what you think. It's something else, but I have a feeling you'll enjoy it."

I slump back into my seat and mope for the rest of the assembly. I don't clap or cheer or even smile with no teeth. I can't believe I will be so close to the secret about unicorns and so far away from it at the same time.

CHAPTER 8

The Most Awful Friday: Part 2

'm sorry we couldn't save you a seat, but we took the last two open ones in the row," Daisy tells me on the way to class after the assembly. The rain has slowed to a drizzle that is more like a mist than rain. Now, instead of using our umbrellas, we are getting wet. (I have noticed that getting wet is one of those things that is superfun to kids and not superfun to adults. This is the reason we dance in the rain and run through sprinklers whenever possible.)

I shrug. There's really nothing to say about it now. The hurt digs itself into my side like a tiny thorn in a cougar's paw. It won't keep me from the rest of my day, but it won't go away either.

"I finished the mustang book last night." Jessica is always the first person done with our book club reads. She completes at least three new books every week. She sighs. "It wasn't as exciting as *From the Mixed-Up Files of Mrs. Basil E. Frankweiler* though."

I have been known to have ideas just pop into my head at the weirdest moments. Someone will say something like, "It's sunny today," and that comment will cause me to think of a way out of a tricky situation. This is exactly what happens now.

Because I know how to visit the Lavender Lakewood exhibit.

I'm going to escape.

I would like to say that I begin to plan my Great Escape (which is what I am calling it to myself) right away. But I have to be patient, like Claudia, and make my plans properly. One does not plot out a museum escape without tremendous thought and a little help.

So first I take my spelling test, which is pretty OK except for this word *reminisce*. It means to remember something with happy feelings. I just can't remember if there is a *c* after the *s*. I write it both ways.

reminisce

reminise

It definitely looks better with the *c* than without it. I decide to go with the *c* version. My cursive *s* isn't the best because it sits sideways too much and tips into the *c* like a floppy teddy bear that can't sit up straight.

After the test is over, I am supposed to go outside with the other fourth- and fifth-grade yard guards and help the first, second, and third graders at playtime or lunch. Siri and I used to be on the playtime shift, but this month, we are helping at lunch. Usually, this is the best part of my Friday, but at the moment, it's not so appealing because Siri is my yard guard partner.

I quickly look to my right to see if Siri is struggling with this idea too. She is looking down at her empty desk with her mouth all scrunched up like she's sick or something. Suddenly, I get so worried that I completely forget all about the Shun and reach out to touch her hand.

"Are you OK?"

Siri looks at me then. Her eyes are filled with tears. They start to spill out of her eyes and run down her cheeks. She quickly wipes her sleeve across her face, so almost no one would know what just happened. I might even think I imagined it except that the shine of tears is still on her face, even though the drops are hidden in her sweat-shirt sleeve.

She doesn't answer, so I ask her another question. "Do you want me to get our yard guard badges?" Whatever the problem is, we can sort through it much better outside the classroom.

Siri nods. I hurry to the drawer for our

red-and-white badges. Mrs. Sablinsky has already excused us, so I don't have to do anything else except put one badge around my neck and hand the other to Siri.

Siri follows me out the door and down the stairs without a word. I think this might be one of those situations where she needs time to open up.

But I am wrong. I am very wrong.

At the bottom of the stairs, Siri turns to me. The tears are gone, and her eyes are bright, like sparks are going to shoot out of them.

The words burst from her like an explosion. "You didn't vote for a new book for next week!"

"You're still mad at me about that?" I don't understand why this has her so upset. She's going to have to explain it to me better than this.

"You don't understand why it's important to me to have book club?"

I think back to yesterday at lunch. So much has happened since then that it seems like a week ago instead of twenty-four hours. I remember Siri saying it would be too late if we didn't choose a new book for next week. "You said to forget it."

"Well, maybe I didn't mean it."

"Wait a minute. You didn't want me to forget it, even though that's what you said?" I knew this was something I needed to remember, even if I didn't understand what I was supposed to remember. We are almost at the lunch tables, and the younger grades are eating. I can see one student having trouble opening a bag of carrots and dip. "Hold on," I say. I dash over and open the package of carrots. I poke a straw through a box of rice milk. I even tie a shoe. I am back to Siri in a superhero flash.

"But book club isn't even your favorite activity. Why is choosing a new book this week so important?"

Siri bursts into tears. She's sobbing as if her heart is breaking into tiny pieces that can't ever be put back together again. I have never seen her like this—never once in six years.

I put my arms around my friend and hold on to her. "If reading a book together means so much to you, then we'll choose one. We can vote today." I am saying what I can to help. Siri starts sniffling now. She pulls away from me, and I see that she's got tears and nose goo everywhere. She wipes her nose on her sweatshirt sleeve.

I step back to the lunch tables. "Can I borrow this?" I ask a small first grader with a paper napkin. It might have some cheese puff dust on it, but otherwise it's clean. I hand the napkin to Siri.

She wipes her nose and then crumples the napkin. "It's not about the book. Not really. It's the Unicorns." I still don't understand. "It will be our last chance to read something together because I'm changing schools." Siri says this like it's a really big deal. But we're fifth graders.

"We're all changing schools—but not for

months. We'll have time to read three or four more books before then." I pat her arm gently. "We get to graduate and everything. It might be confusing at first to be in middle school and have six classes instead of one. I'm sure we'll get the hang of it as long as we're together."

Siri shakes her head and wipes her nose again on the now very crumpled and used napkin. "That's the thing—we won't be together." She takes a shaky breath in. "I'm switching to a different school but not next year. Now. Well, not now-now. In January."

My first reaction to this news is to blink a bunch of times super-duper fast. This is because I think I might be having one of my imagination bubbles. There is no possible way this can really and truly be happening.

When the bubble doesn't pop, I know this is real. Siri is still crying, even though it's softer now.

"My dad likes this other middle school, and

it's in a different school district that has a lottery. The best way to increase my chances of getting in is to move to the elementary school now." She lets out a big breath like she's been holding it for a really long time and can finally breathe normally again. "I'm sorry."

My hands are sweaty, and my throat is dry like it is at the dentist's office after a cleaning, when I have had to hold it open for thirty minutes. Siri is leaving school. Worse even than that—we won't be going to the same middle school.

My mind jumps ahead to high school because middle school is only three years. If we aren't at the same middle school, what are the chances we will be at the same high school? And if we aren't at the same high school, will we go to the same college and have our New York apartment? Suddenly, my entire life plan has been altered with one sentence (or maybe two)—I can't remember if Siri told me with one complete sentence or a sentence and a fragment. Why am I thinking about grammar at a time like this?!

I notice that Siri is staring at me. I open my mouth to say something, but nothing comes out. All I get is a sound between a creak and a croak. I sit down right there on the ground and stare straight ahead.

I am not me. I am a frog sitting alone on a lily pad in a pond.
I used to have a lot of frog friends, but all of them have
hopped away to a fancier pond with red dragonflies, pink
swans, and golden geese. Now I am left with just one teeny
fly to talk to and a flamingo with mismatched socks. Neither
one of them speaks ribbit.

"We will still be besties even if we aren't at the same school," Siri offers. I am supposed to be cheering her up, but she is doing the cheering now. I know perfectly well that she is saying one of those things you say to make someone feel better even if it isn't the truth.

That's why I stand up and brush myself off. "There's nothing we can do about it, right?" I ask.

Siri shakes her head no.

(In stories, sometimes the main characters have to go their separate ways. They always come back together in the end. Friends like us have a forever kind of bond.)

That's why I link my arm in Siri's and finish our yard guard shift. The Shun is as forgotten as the crumpled napkin Siri tosses into the trash.

CHAPTER 9

Escaping with a Plan

At lunch, Siri tells the other Unicorns the truth. It's definitely the saddest lunch we've ever shared. There are more tears—and a few runny noses.

"We can make a promise to have an annual sleepover every year during winter break," Charlotte suggests.

"We can also move the Unicorn Book Club meetings to Saturday afternoons," I offer. I'm sure my mom would let me have my best friends over to talk about books.

"What if we pass around a journal and each write something that has happened to us in it?

Then we can keep sharing experiences with each other," Daisy says.

We all have ideas to keep our group connected. Even as good as the ideas are, they still don't change the fact that Siri won't be here to be my yard guard partner or my running buddy or to eat lunch with me. The Unicorns will be missing a member. I'm not really sure if a weekend book club will work. My lunch sits unopened for the second time this week.

Siri rubs her eyes with another borrowed napkin. "Can we change the subject?"

Everyone nods, but no one has any idea what to say. My mind is going over all the things that will be different without Siri here.

She turns to me then. "Ruby, any book news?"

I do have something to talk about, and with everything else that has happened, I almost forgot. "The book I'm reading is about a researcher who searched for unicorns in the world. I think she might have found one, but the clues are hidden in her research, and no one else has ever been able to discover the unicorn."

I look around to see if my friends are interested in hearing more. They are all eating their lunches and listening to me. So I continue. "I found out that there is an exhibit with her notes at the Natural History Museum!"

I expect my friends to be excited about this news—and they are. There is so much chatter about unicorns and the exhibit that I almost can't bring myself to tell them the bad news about it. "I asked Mrs. Sablinsky if we could see the exhibit next week, and she said there won't be time."

There is a chorus of "awwww" and "no way" from my friends. Daisy even makes her sad, puppy-dog face. I know how to see the exhibit—but I will need help to do it.

I always make big announcements in two parts, so I begin with:

"I think I know how we can go anyway,

even if Mrs. Sablinsky won't let us." All eyes are on me.

"We'll run away from the field trip."

Jessica catches on right away. "Sort of like *From the Mixed-Up Files*."

"But *our* version," Siri adds with a sparkly smile at me.

"It's a real mystery!" Charlotte is super-excited.

Daisy doesn't look so sure. "We might get in trouble."

"We also might get away with it," Charlotte whispers as she passes out square cheese crackers.

"But how?" Jessica asks as she eats the cracker in one bite. She crunches as she waits for me to answer.

"Like Claudia—with expert planning," I answer.

By the time the bell rings for the end of lunch, we have all agreed: next Thursday will be the day of the Great Museum Escape.

In class, we have time to do research on the computer for our book reports. I decide to look up the layout of the Natural History Museum.

I draw out my own map and track where the class will be going with little footprints. I know from Mrs. S that the class will be seeing mammals, insects, and dinosaurs. Then there will be a surprise. I can't tell whether that will be the whale exhibit or the butterfly pavilion. Just in case, I mark both areas. Next, I plan an escape route. The main issue will be timing. If we leave school for the museum at 8:30 a.m. and arrive at the museum by 9:15 a.m., we will have exactly three hours in which to escape, visit Lavender Lakewood's exhibit, decipher her codes, and return to the class tour before lunchtime.

Three hours might not be enough time to figure out a mystery that has stumped even the world's smartest historians and researchers. I decide that the best plan is for us to come up with a few theories before the museum visit. That way, we will already be prepared with options.

On my map, I include all the halls and exhibits as well as the main entrance and emergency exits (it's always a good idea to be prepared), restrooms, the restaurant, and the gift shop.

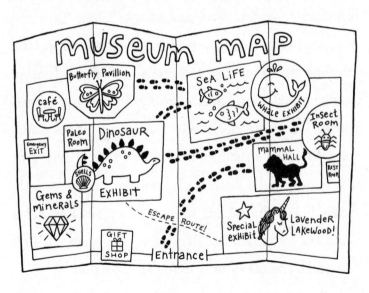

The last part of our day is spent with quiet reading time—more Lavender Lakewood for me! I open volume two, the one with her field notes, and start reading:

I begin by assembling notes from researchers before me. Then I look at other creatures like the unicorn. Wild horses and deer are a good place to start. I move into the forest and set up camp. There, I begin to think like a unicorn. As a prey animal, the unicorn must rely on its own courage, ability to camouflage, and quick thinking to protect itself. I begin to track through the forests of Europe one at a time. I look for areas of dense coverage, available water, and generous amounts of sunlight.

Mom is waiting for me outside of school. "How was your day?" she asks right away.

"Not so good," I tell her. "I found out that Siri is moving schools in January."

Mom knows better than to have this conversation in front of school. She just slings my backpack over her arm and takes my hand in hers. Once we are in the car though, she wants the whole story. I tell her all of it, even the part where I voted against Siri in book club before I understood that reading one last book together was really important to her.

"I'm sorry to hear about Siri. She's been your friend for a long time, and I know how much you'll miss her." She is at a stoplight, so she turns around to the backseat to look right at me. "It sounds like it will be a hard time for both of you."

"I don't think we will want to have a book club without her," I say over the grumble of my stomach. I've really missed a lot of meals lately. I think I'll have to make up for it this weekend. Maybe I can ask Mom to make veggie burgers and fries.

"You could have meetings on the weekends," Mom suggests. "It would be a nice way to see each other."

"We thought about that too." Meetings on the weekends wouldn't be the same. But there would be one good thing that could come out of it. "At least there wouldn't be any food fights ending our meetings early."

"That's true. But Abe might join your group. Are you open to dog members?" Mom stops the car at a red light. She looks over her shoulder again to smile at me.

I want to smile with her, but I am not in a smiling mood. Here is the question that has been in my mind since Siri told me she was switching schools: "Do you think Siri and I will stay friends?"

"If she is important enough to you, then you will make sure the friendship lasts."

"She is important to me," I answer.

"I know," Mom says softly. Neither one of us says anything after that. The words just kind of drift in the air like a swirly, blue fog.

Mom parks at the grocery store. Sometimes

★ ★ 147 ★ ★

we stop for a few things before we get Sam and Connor. I have something else to say though.

"I thought I knew how everything was going to be, and now I don't. It makes me feel like I fell down Alice's rabbit hole." I take a big breath because the tears that are filling my eyes are somehow making my breath come in bursts. (How is it that tiny tears can be so powerful?)

She turns around in her seat to look at me. "Ruby, there are some things in life that we can't control. This is one of them. You can't change the decision Siri's family has made. But you can make your own decisions." Mom hands me a tissue.

"Like what?" I sniffle. I have to admit that I am in full crying mode now.

"Deciding to continue being Siri's friend. Deciding to keep your book club together. Opening your heart to making new friends."

"I can do all that," I tell her.

"I know you can," Mom says as she touches her finger to my nose.

When I get out of the car, I wrap my arms around Mom and hold on tight. Sometimes a hug is better than words—and this is one of those times.

Saturday morning is spent on holiday crafting. Mom gets out all these different ribbons, shapes made out of wood, and paints in every color. Then, we sit at the kitchen table and make picture frames and bulletin boards. The frames are easy because all we do is paint and glue the wood pieces into rectangle shapes. The bulletin boards are a little more complicated. First, we cover the wood in a fabric, and then we criss-cross ribbons on the board to make little diamond shapes. We wrap the ribbons around the edges of the wood, and Mom staples them to the back.

Pictures will fit underneath the ribbons and stay on the board.

I think Mom asked me to craft with her this morning to take my mind off of Siri leaving school. She even turns on the radio so we can listen to the oldies station while we work. But no matter what I am doing, my heart aches. In a few weeks, I will have to say goodbye to my best friend. I know it's not forever, but it feels like it is. Maybe my other friends will change schools too. Then I will be left all alone like one of those sneakers you sometimes see in the middle of the street. Once or twice, I've even spotted a sneaker hanging from the top of a telephone pole. I don't know how the sneaker got there, but I do know that the one shoe looks really lonely without its other half.

Crafting is hard work. By the time we're finished, I'm ready for lunch. Mom makes peanut butter and jelly sandwiches with cut-up green apples on the side. Yum! (Confession time: I love green apples almost as much as I love pickles.) Abe sits underneath the table, of course, but he pokes his nose out from time to time, just to remind us that he is here. Abe is a big fan of peanut butter.

Sam eats lunch with us. Connor and Dad have gone out to the hardware store to get supplies for one of Connor's science projects, so it's just the three of us (and Abe).

Sam talks about his cookie flavors. "I'm thinking of cranberry-coconut sugar cookies, chocolate-peppermint cookies, or lemon drop cookies. What do you think?"

I love anything coconut, so usually I would vote for those. But the lemon drops sound way more unusual. "If you were on a baking show, I would say lemon drops would get the judges' attention."

Sam nods. "You're right. They would add something different though, like basil or cinnamon."

Mom grins at me. "I bet Ruby would add pickles."

I laugh. "I would! They go with everything."

Sam shakes his head. He isn't as obsessed with pickles. "I'm going to skip pickles this time. No offense." He finishes his second peanut butter sandwich. "But I think I will add honey to the cookies."

"That sounds delicious. I can't wait to try them," Mom says. I help her clear the plates from the table. Abe follows along behind me, hoping I accidentally drop one of the plates. (I don't.)

"Would you videotape me, so I can practice speaking on camera?" Sam asks me.

"I'd love to!" is my answer. I borrow Dad's video camera and hurry back to the kitchen. Sam measures out all the ingredients and puts them in a line on the counter in clear glass bowls. It looks super-professional. He's like a TV chef already!

"When you're finished, I'll make my chocolate chip cookies," Mom tells us. "I could use a helper."

"You can count on me," I promise. I love baking chocolate chip cookies. Mom always lets me sample the chocolate chips before we add them into the cookie batter.

"I think it's time for Abe and me to take a walk," Mom says. The minute Abe hears the word *walk*, he runs over to the kitchen door and starts whining. Mom can't get the leash fast enough for him. He spins around in circles and jumps up on the door.

Mom waves to us from the doorway. "The kitchen's all yours."

I stand across the counter from my brother, so I can see his face and his hands while he mixes the ingredients. He's really good at the talking part. He says things like, "First, you want to measure out your dry ingredients. Next, mix them together in a large bowl and set it aside," and, "Preheat the oven to 350 degrees. The cookies will bake evenly if you cover your pan with parchment paper dusted with flour." I watch as my brother cracks the eggs with one hand and doesn't even get one drop on the counter.

"You're as good as one of the bakers on *Cupcake Champions*!" I tell Sam. "Only you're a cookie champion."

When he's all finished and the cookies come out of the oven, the whole house smells like lemonade and sugar cookies. Here are my top three favorite smells:

1. New books
2. Libraries
3. Freshly baked cookies

Sam and I sit down to try one of the warm cookies. The rest are for Gram's cookie party tomorrow.

"Did any of your good friends ever switch

schools?" I ask him. I can't remember this ever happening to him, but I ask anyway.

Sam cuts the cookie in half. "I had one friend that went to a different middle school for a year. Then he came back because he didn't like the other school. I knew someone else who switched to a different high school for a year too. She returned this year." We each take a bite. Mmmmm! It's tangy and sugary.

"It's so delicious!" I tell him. "This might be the best cookie I've ever tasted."

"Thanks," he says with a grin. "I hope Gram likes them." Then he gets serious. "Siri might not stay at the other school. You never know what will happen in the future. All you can do is focus on today." I could listen to my brother and only focus on today—or I could change the future. I think I know the perfect way to do it.

CHAPTER 10

The Unicorn Seekers

Monday morning, I hurry to find Siri. "I have a plan," I say as part one of my signature two-part announcement. Then I tell her part two: "We are going to become world-famous Unicorn Seekers."

"I'll still have to go to a different school in January," Siri points out.

I shake my head. That's the perfection of my plan. "You won't have to go to school at all! None of us will. We'll be traveling all over the world giving speeches and sharing our research. And we'll be together!"

Siri claps her hands together. "Unicorn

Siri and I are in an empty white room with three doors. In my hand, I hold one of her teardrops. All her sadness is in this one single tear. In Siri's hand, she holds one of my teardrops. All of my sadness is in that tear. In the room, there are three doors—one red, one blue, and one green. I open the blue door, and outside, we can see an ocean of tears. Siri and I gently slip the teardrops into the ocean. We watch as our teardrops float away.

Seekers! I like it. I can even design special outfits for us when we give our speeches."

After a lesson in social studies, we have time in the library for more reading and research. Mrs. S likes our reports to be completed at school, so our parents won't be taking over and writing the papers for us. I know I should be working on my paper. I have two whole books to read. But instead, I meet with the Unicorns at the back table and discuss our plan.

"If we find the last unicorn, then we will be too famous to go to school. We can stay together and write books and visit museums. School won't be important anymore."

"Who is going to travel with us?" Daisy asks. "My mom won't let me go to the store by myself. I'm guessing traveling to London or Paris would be a definite no."

I have it all figured out. "My grandma can be our chaperone. She loves to travel."

The Unicorns like that idea. The group chatter starts up now. I have to settle everyone down. This must be the way Mrs. S feels on a Friday after assembly. It's hard to get everyone's attention focused. "We can't get famous if we don't actually find the unicorn. Keeping Siri with us depends on solving the mystery. And that all begins on the field trip. We have to work out how to escape to the exhibit."

My friends are all looking at me now. No one is talking anymore. I have brought my map with me, so I pull it out of my jeans pocket and unfold it on the table. "I made this, so we can plan our escape. Here is where I think the class will be going." I point to the mammal hall. "After that, we are going here." I trace my finger along the path to the insect room. "We'll have to escape when the class goes to see the dinosaurs."

"I wanted to see the dinosaurs," Jessica says with a little frown.

I understand. I want to see the dinosaurs too. "We might make it back in time. If we solve the mystery really quick, it will be like we never left at all."

"Could we leave earlier?" Charlotte wants to know. "Then we won't miss the dinosaurs."

I shake my head. "We can't leave right away. It'll be too obvious. We have to slip away in the middle of the tour."

"How are we going to just walk away from the class?" Siri asks. She is leaning over, studying the map as if the paper has the answer.

I look up to make sure Mrs. Xia and Mrs. S aren't watching us. I see them at the front desk, chatting. I wonder what they would have to talk about—books, maybe, or sensible dinner foods. But I can't get distracted by my imagination right now. I have to plot an escape.

I whisper, "We can get away in groups of two and three." This will be better than all of us leaving at once. It will be less noticeable, anyway.

Jessica looks at Daisy, who nods. "We'll stay together."

"Great," I answer. "Siri and Charlotte and I will be a team then."

"We can ask to go to the bathroom," Siri suggests. "Then we can pretend to walk in the bathroom but really go the other way to the unicorn exhibit."

"And Jessica and Daisy can take extra time looking at one of the exhibits and drop behind," I add. "Then they can slip out of the exhibit and meet us." This could work. "We might need a lookout though—someone on the inside who isn't trying to leave." I am thinking Will P might be this person.

"We shouldn't involve anyone else. If they told someone, we could get in big trouble," Charlotte warns.

If that happened, we might not even get to

go on the field trip at all. This makes me realize that I need to say something to the group. "Here's the thing: I don't want you to feel like you have to do this with me. It's really important that I get the chance to see Lavender's notes in person. But I don't want anyone to get in trouble." This kind of trouble is the very worst kind: Trouble with a capital *T*. This is *principal's office, call your parents* kind of trouble. And not one of us has ever been in the principal's office except for good reasons, like to ask for permission to have a bake sale (but that's a whole other story). "You can still be seekers with me, so you can be famous and leave school and everything."

"I'm going with you," Siri promises.

"Me too," Charlotte adds.

Jessica nods. "I want to solve the mystery too."

"I could be your lookout," Daisy says in a small voice. "I really don't want to separate from the class."

"But then you won't be there when we find the last unicorn. Would you mind?" I ask.

"Not at all," she says.

"You'll still be one of the Unicorn Seekers," Siri tells her as she throws an arm around Daisy's shoulder.

"Good," she says with a grin. "I want to go to Paris."

I nod. "Paris will be the first place we give one of our speeches. Then we can visit Scotland. I think there might still be dragons there. Maybe we can find one."

"We'll be dragon and unicorn seekers," Charlotte announces in a very un-library voice. I look over at Mrs. S to see if she has noticed. But she is still busy with her chitchat. Now she is even waving her hands in the air for emphasis. It must be a very exciting subject.

I look around the table at my friends. "We'll be in two groups then. Siri and I will leave first.

Charlotte and Jessica, you two will leave second. Daisy will keep watch. If we can get away during the dinosaurs, then I think we will have until the surprise part, which should be right before lunchtime. I'm thinking the surprise will be either here"—I point to the whale exhibit—"or here." I show them the butterfly exhibit.

"I definitely don't want to miss butterflies," Siri admits.

Me either. "We will be sure to make it back for that part." That reminds me of something. "We probably need a watch. Time can really speed up when you are on an adventure." I know this from reading lots of books where the main character has to be a hero. Heroes definitely do not pay attention to the clock.

I lean close to my friends and drop my voice to a whisper. You never know when someone is listening. "Claudia prepared for every situation, and even though we aren't exactly running away, I think we should be ready. Planning is everything."

"I have a tiny flashlight that fits in my pocket," Jessica offers.

I nod. "Perfect. Anyone else?"

Charlotte speaks up next. "I can bring some extra snacks, just in case we don't get back by lunchtime."

"I have a digital camera," Siri shares. "We might want to take pictures of something we see."

"Good thinking," I say with a grin. My friends are really good seekers. "I'll bring paper and a pen for taking notes."

"Claudia and her brother Jamie brought extra clothes. Maybe you should all wear extra sweatshirts, just in case it's cold in there." Daisy wraps her arms around herself as if she is already in the shadows.

That gets me thinking. What if we do get separated and can't find our way back? We might have to spend the night in the museum. A whole night there should be enough time to find the secret clues in the exhibit. "If we can't find our way back to the class, we will have to be prepared to spend the night."

Charlotte wrinkles her nose like she has just smelled salami. "Mrs. Sablinsky would notice if four of us were missing. She would worry about us." Charlotte is a big fan of Mrs. Sablinsky. I always think that's because she started school in October. I've known Mrs. S for two more months than Charlotte. I guess Mrs. S would notice if we were missing, but I'm not so sure she would be worried—I think she would be seriously annoyed. "What if she couldn't find us? What then?"

"We'd have more time to look for clues," Jessica answers with a grin.

I look around at my friends. They need to understand how important our quest has become. This is about more than my book report. It's about

I am in the Natural History Museum with Siri, Jessica,
Charlotte, and Daisy. It is late at night and we are all alone
in the dark. The animal shapes make giant, monster-sized
shadows on the walls. The lions seem to be watching us.
Daisy is sure that the hyenas are alive. Jessica shines her
flashlight around the room to find us someplace safe to sleep.
All we can see are animal teeth. In one of the exhibits, I
spot a giant bird nest. We all climb in and cover up with our
sweatshirts. The giant bird doesn't look happy to see us taking
over her nest, especially since we use her eggs as pillows.

more than Lavender Lakewood's mystery. "We have to find the missing unicorn. This is to save Siri."

"What will we actually do when we get to the Lavender Lakewood exhibit?" Charlotte asks.

That's something I have wondered about myself. (Sometimes the hero in the story has to trust her instincts about what to do next.)

"Claudia and Jamie had to fit clues together to find the real answer about Angel," I say, thinking out loud. "It was visiting Mrs. Basil E. Frankweiler that made all the difference though."

"Can we visit Lavender Lakewood?" Jessica asks.

I shake my head. "She wrote the books in the 1920s. She would be more than one hundred years old if she was still alive." I really am a math whiz! "And she lived in England."

Charlotte leans her head on her arm and sighs. "Then we can't visit her or even write her a letter."

I shake my head. "We will have to figure this out on our own, like Nancy Drew."

Nancy always looks carefully at all the clues. The clues hold the answers to the mystery. We can do this—I know we can.

"Maybe if we shine Jessica's flashlight on the original notes, the light will reveal a hidden map," I suggest. My best ideas come from the pages of books I have read. In one story, the hero found a map by shining the light from a candle on a very old letter. The map was drawn with invisible ink.

"Oh, that's a really good idea, Ruby." Jessica's eyes are bright with excitement.

"Or maybe there is a code using letters," Siri offers. "Like one of Mrs. Sablinsky's math pages."

Mrs. Sablinsky loves to give math homework with codes. Here's how it works: At the top of the page is a riddle. In the middle of the page are division or multiplication problems. Each answer matches a letter and the letters spell the word or words that solve the riddle.

Who knew math homework could help us find a unicorn?

"You're right." I grin at Siri. "We're experts at breaking codes."

Daisy leans in close. "If we could see the original notes, maybe we could find the answer there."

I fold up the map and put it back into my pocket before Mrs. Xia or Mrs. Sablinsky notices. Explaining why we have a map of the Natural History Museum would not be easy.

I look around at the Unicorns and I know I couldn't ask for better or smarter friends. We're ready. Now all we have to do is wait until Thursday and hope none of us get the stomach flu and have to miss the field trip.

CHAPTER 11

The One and Only Great Museum Escape

The week is maybe the fastest week of my entire life because before I know it, Thursday morning has arrived.

I have read both of Lavender's books and written most of my report. The good thing about looking for clues to the location of the last unicorn is that everything I've learned can go into my paper. When you really know your subject, it's easy to write about it. I am a teensy bit nervous though—not about escaping from the field trip. I'm nervous that I will finally be looking at the real research, and I won't be able to solve the mystery.

I may have read a lot of mysteries, but I am not a real sleuth, no matter how much I wish I were.

We line up in front of the bus. The class is super-loud because we are all excited. I can only compare it to the volume dial on Dad's car radio. It seems like someone has turned the volume up as high as it can go on the students of Room 15.

For some reason, we stand in line for a really, really long time. Mrs. Sablinsky is talking to one of the other fifth grade teachers and the parent chaperones. Will P's mother is the chaperone for our class. It was supposed to be a random selection, but I'm sure that Will being Mrs. Sablinsky's favorite student of all time probably had a lot to do with it.

I wish Mrs. Sablinsky would hurry up and let us get onto the bus. The sooner we arrive, the sooner we can escape.

Siri and I both have our lunches in paper

tote bags. Charlotte, Jessica, and Daisy have old-school paper sacks.

"Do you have the flashlight?" I whisper to Jessica.

She nods and points to her belt loop. There on a key chain hangs a little blue flashlight.

"Did you bring the pen and paper?" Charlotte asks me. I unzip my sweatshirt to show my friends my shirt with a pocket. Inside the pocket, I have a small pen and two folded sheets of paper.

Charlotte grins. "That's good thinking." Then she points to her dress pockets. "I brought five granola bars and three fruit strips. That's all I could fit in here."

Siri rolls back her sweater sleeve. There, she has the digital camera strap around her wrist.

"Where's the camera?" Daisy wants to know. I can't see it either.

"Right here," Siri announces. Then she

shows us that she has tucked the camera inside her sleeve.

"It's much smaller than I expected." I have never seen such a tiny digital camera.

"I know, right?" Siri is beaming like she invented the camera herself. I can't help but smile with her. It's actually pretty great to see her happy. "And it takes amazing pictures."

All of a sudden, I think I understand how my mom feels when she looks at me and my brothers. Because I am really proud of my friends. We might actually be able to escape after all.

"I have the map in my shoe," I share in a whisper. "It seemed safer than in my pocket. I'll take it out once we get there."

Just then, Mrs. Sablinsky walks to the front of our line. Finally!

"You will be split into two groups," she tells us. "One group will be with me and one group will be with Mrs. Pasternak." She points to Will's mom. "I will assign your group once we arrive at the museum."

"I hope we're with Mrs. Pasternak," Siri whispers. "It will be a lot easier to escape from someone who doesn't know us."

I nod. "That's true." I hold up my crossed fingers. (Crossing your fingers might not really bring good luck, but we can use all the help we can get today.) "Just remember not to talk about the Great Escape once we are on the bus."

I think about what Mrs. S just said. I didn't realize our class would be split into groups. What if my friends and I are separated? Then we might not be in the dinosaur exhibit at the same time. If we aren't there at the same time, we won't be able to escape together. Then our plan can't possibly work. I don't have time to talk to the other Unicorns though, because the line moves forward. We are actually getting on the bus.

Siri asked Charlotte to be seat partners

during the Shun, so I am still facing the ride partnerless. My friends are ahead of me, and they are already in their seats when I climb up the three stairs into the bus. For someone who has been partnerless on a bus ride, this will be nothing unexpected. For someone who hasn't been partnerless on a bus ride, it's like this: everywhere you look, people are in pairs. The pairs are staring like they know you are partnerless. The back of your neck begins to heat up, and your mouth gets dry. You just want to sit down, but you don't know where to go. It's awful.

I slide into the first empty seat I can find, which is in front of Jessica and Daisy and across from Siri and Charlotte. It's a supergood thing we decided not to talk about the Great Escape on the bus, since guess who decides to sit with me. Mrs. Sablinsky! I never would have predicted that!

On the bus, my friends talk and laugh. They play guessing games. In other words, they have a great time. But I just sit there because I can't think of one single thing to say to my teacher besides telling her that I can't wait to get there (which I say twice). A bus ride is not nearly as much fun when you aren't sitting next to a friend. Also, it seems to go on forever. It's like that baby song about bus wheels that keep going around and around. This bus ride just keeps going and going. Are we driving to New York?

Then, the worst thing ever happens: the thing I never could have predicted. And there is absolutely nothing I can do about it. I get... *bus sick.*

For those of you who have never experienced this horrific state, congratulations. You are very lucky. For the rest of us, it's that queasy, headachy, want-to-go-to-sleep state that lasts for hours.

By the time we reach the front of the Natural History Museum, I am sure my skin is the color of a gecko. I actually think my tongue might even be sweating. In other words, I am completely and totally miserable.

How in the world am I going to execute our grand adventure like this?

That's when the unexpected happens: Mrs. Sablinsky notices. Well, of course she notices. I am greener than the Wicked Witch of the West.

"Ruby, did you get motion sick?"

It is nearly impossible to speak in this condition, partly because the bumpy bump of the bus is still pounding in my head and partly because, if I open my mouth, my breakfast might be coming back out.

"Try this." She gives me a little lemon candy and a bottle of water. I eat the candy and surprise! It actually helps. She hands me a second one. "It's one of my tricks. My sister gets terrible motion sickness, so I'm always prepared."

Mrs. S has a sister. Who knew?

I stand there gulping fresh air and hoping my

plan will still work as my teacher begins to lead the class through the doors of the museum. The Unicorns stay together near the back of the group. If our plan is going to work, the two twosomes need to be in the same group.

Once we step through the doors, I check the surroundings. My map is exactly right. The calculations leave us escaping while the class is in the dinosaur exhibit. Then, we will rejoin at the whale exhibit or butterfly pavilion. (I have to admit that I hope we make it back in time for butterflies. I have always wanted to be in one of those enclosures with all the colorful wings floating around me.)

Mrs. Sablinsky passes out little, orange stickers for all of us. I put the sticker on my sweatshirt. Then she holds up her class roster. "Please listen for your name. I will be calling out group one first. You will be with Mrs. Pasternak."

Mrs. Pasternak stands over to the side with a wide smile on her face. She looks a lot like Will, except that her glasses are blue instead of red. Also, she doesn't have on funny socks.

I hear my teacher call out a lot of names: "Will B, Bryden, Jason, Will P." But I don't hear my name or my friends' names. This is a good thing because we are all in the same group. It's a bad thing because...

"If I haven't read your name, you will be in my group."

We're with Mrs. Sablinsky. Escaping from our teacher's group will be way more complicated than escaping from Will P's mom. But it will have to be done.

"No turning back now," I whisper to my friends as we gather together in front of Mrs. Sablinsky.

A young man dressed in a tan explorer's outfit joins us. "Hi, everyone. I'm Joe, and I will be guiding you through the Natural History Museum today. First, we will be traveling to Africa to see the land mammals. Everyone ready to start on the journey?"

Exactly as I predicted, we head to the mammal hall first. The giant sign reads AFRICA and shows where different animals can be found there. Once we pass the sign, I see that the entire room is filled with glass cases with animals inside. There is something super-creepy about them. I think they might be real dead animals that someone stuffed.

"Here you will find the predators and prey animals from Africa." Joe keeps talking, but I don't hear him. I am too busy looking at the ginormous lion. Are they really that big? The lion faces three zebras like it is going to pounce on them any second. For a minute, I forget that it isn't alive. Daisy grabs my arm and points to the hyenas, which are watching us like they can read our minds.

"They're staring at me!" Daisy whispers.

"They probably wish they could get out of here. Don't look at them," I advise her, and I do the same. We hurry to catch up to our friends, who are touching different animal bones. Siri tries to pass one to me. I shake my head. I'm ready to leave this area and get on with our escape. Siri doesn't realize that I don't want it, so she hands it to me. Only I don't know she is handing it to me, which is a really long way of saying: I drop the animal bone. Or rather, Siri drops it. But it seems like I have dropped it.

When you drop something at school, like a pencil or a book, it doesn't make a noticeable sound. Also, the classroom is usually pretty noisy. When you drop something at a museum, now, that is a whole different story. The bone clangs onto the marble floor and echoes in the room full of dead animals. Every head snaps in my direction. My teacher pinches her lips together in her "I am not happy, not at all" face. Meanwhile, my face has turned flaming red. I can't see my face of course, because there aren't any mirrors in the African savannah. But I know it's red because it gets superhot like I've been running the mile on a May afternoon.

"Sorry," I whisper. I lean over to pick up the bone, but Joe gets there faster.

"These things happen," he tells me with a smile. Mrs. Sablinsky is not so forgiving. She narrows her eyes and glares at me. This is not good. Not good at all. I wanted to be invisible during the field trip. I didn't want to be on my teacher's radar. Now it will be that much harder to get away.

Joe leads us to a giant giraffe. This one is outside of the case, so we can stand next to it and see how tall it is. One by one, we are supposed to step onto a circle near the front left leg of the giraffe, and Joe will take our picture.

"Can we go together?" Charlotte asks Joe.

"Sure you can," he answers.

So that's how the Unicorns take a picture of our first big escape together (pre-escape, of course). I'm on the end so I put my right arm around Siri's shoulders. She puts her left arm around my shoulders and her right one around Charlotte who is next to her. Then Charlotte links with Siri and Daisy. Daisy continues the chain with Jessica who is on the other end. We are a big pretzel of arms and laughter, because for some reason, we can't stop giggling. It's really hard to stand in a line with your arms twisted and laugh at the same time. We teeter from side to side and we are halfway to tipping over when Joe calls out: "Say giraffe!"

I am one hundred percent certain that "giraffe" doesn't work as well as saying "cheese" when someone takes your photo. My mouth moves open instead of sideways. It doesn't really matter though, because it is one of those special moments that I know I will always remember.

"That might have been our last school picture together." Siri bites her lip like she's trying to keep from saying more. We step away to let other students take their photos.

I shake my head. "Don't think like that. We're on a mission today, and when we succeed, you won't have to worry about school at all."

The mammal tour seems to be taking a lot longer than expected. I thought we would zip through this room and move on to insects. But now Joe is taking us toward a giant cutout of California.

"Here we will see the mammals that are native to our great state."

My friends and I are lagging behind the group, so we can talk without our teacher hearing us. "This is taking forever," I whisper.

"We might have to change our plan," Jessica responds in a hushed voice.

"We don't want to miss our chance," Siri adds.

"I changed my mind about being a lookout. I'd rather come with you." Daisy looks around the room with her eyes wide. "I'll have nightmares for weeks after this."

"Then the Great Museum Escape begins now," I announce. "Everyone ready?"

My friends nod.

The real adventure is about to begin.

CHAPTER 12

It's All About the Plan

M ay I please go to the restroom?" I'm the one to ask Mrs. Sablinsky the question that will begin our escape.

Since I was sick from the bus ride, I am thinking I have a pretty good chance of being excused. "Yes, but please take a buddy with you."

"Siri, can you come with me?" I am so smooth that I actually surprise myself.

"Sure," she says with a smile big enough to show her pink braces.

"The restrooms are just outside this hall and to the right," Mrs. S tells us. "Come right back. We should be moving through the rest of the mammals and then going to see the insects."

"Thank you," I say to my teacher. It's always a good idea to be polite, especially when you are about to completely and totally break the rules.

"Unicorn," I whisper to Charlotte as I pass her.

"Unicorn," Jessica says to Siri.

This is our code word for the escape: *unicorn* (which is pretty perfect if you ask me).

Siri and I link hands, and I have to hold in a little squeal of excitement. We're really doing this!

Outside the mammal hall and to the right is the restroom. I can see the blue sign directly ahead. The plan is in full swing. Here we go...

"I think I'll go with you," Mrs. Sablinsky says just behind me and over my shoulder.

Noooooooooooooooooooooooooooooooooooooooooo!

It can't be happening. But it is. My teacher has just crushed our escape plan. Now, instead of only pretending to go toward the bathroom but then veering back to the Lavender Lakewood exhibit, I am going into the bathroom with my teacher.

Unless I dash out when she is washing her hands, there is no escape for us right now. Siri and I trade looks, and our looks are saying paragraphs.

Details about the bathroom experience are not necessary, except to say that within five minutes, we are following Mrs. S back to the mammal hall. I look over my shoulder at the sign pointing to the special exhibit area. It's exactly where I thought it would be. (I really am an expert mapmaker!) But there is no possible way we can get to it right now.

Siri and I have no choice but to rejoin the class and go to the insect room. The minute our friends see us return with Mrs. S, they know. We all share looks of disappointment. But I'm not ready to give up yet. After all, our original plan was to leave during the dinosaur exhibit. There will still be a chance to get away. I am sure of it.

The bug room is filled with, guess what...

bugs! Only in this area, the creatures are actually alive. I wish Connor were here to see this. Charlotte volunteers to hold a Madagascar hissing cockroach in her hand! I would never, and I mean *never*, hold a cockroach in my hand—no matter what. Ick!

Around us, there are cases with different kinds of spiders (also high on the creepy meter) crawling around. Joe is really excited about this part of the tour. He recites endless bug facts and answers a whole bunch of questions. I would like to attempt another escape, but there is no way Mrs. Sablinsky will let me go to the bathroom again.

"I knew we should have been in the other group," Siri says to me when we are looking into a case with hundreds or maybe thousands of tiny, black ants.

"It would have been way easier. That's for sure." I watch the ants travel through their tunnels.

"Can we try again?" Jessica asks. "Maybe Charlotte and I should go to the bathroom now."

I give Jessica one of my signature winks. "I have a feeling about the dinosaur exhibit. Let's wait until we get there."

When we finally cross through the center of the museum and step into the dinosaur exhibit, I forget about the escape for a minute. Because the bones of the T. rex have been put together so it's life-sized—and it's bigger than a building. I wouldn't want to be living side by side with this guy, that's for sure.

"Wow," Daisy breathes.

"Wow is right," Jessica adds.

My friends and I stand in front of the dinosaur and just stare. For once, words fail me. I can't imagine putting these pieces together. It's like the biggest puzzle in the history of the world.

That's when our luck changes. Because Will P's group comes into the exhibit too. Now our entire class is here. Better than that, there are several other school field trip groups here. The area around the T. rex is swarming with so many kids it reminds me of the ants I just saw in the case. Mrs. S would never notice if we slipped away now.

"Unicorn," I whisper to Siri. She passes it down all the way to Daisy. Then Daisy passes it back. When Siri says, "unicorn," to me, I know we are all ready.

"Follow my lead," I tell her.

It's time for the "drifting away" plan. I pretend to be reading all the paragraphs on the wall. Then I look at the dinosaur eye display. The Unicorns stand side by side and study the map on the wall. But we're not reading. We're waiting for our moment to break away.

When the class turns a corner, I look around and sigh. We are finally all alone. But I'm turned around and mixed up. "I'm not really sure which way to go now." I say softly.

Siri points to the left. "I think it's that way."

"I'm pretty sure it's the other way," Jessica argues.

Now I don't know which way to go for the unicorn exhibit. Then I remember the map in my shoe. I bend down and pull it out. It's folded super-small, so I have to open and open and open before we can look at it. Oh no! All of my pen marks have smeared. The footprints have blended into the words and the exhibits all look like blobs. I can't tell which way to go at all. I stand while I am turning the map upside down and right side up again. That's when I sort of lose my balance. (OK, I completely and totally lose my balance.) I fall through the red velvet ropes around the raptor exhibit.

Yes, it happens—the worst possible thing that could happen happens: I slam right into the skeleton of the raptor.

"Ruby!" someone calls out. I don't have time to look because I am too busy crashing to the floor.

The poles holding the red velvet ropes tip over and make a clanging sound like a gong when they bang against the marble floor. Basically, I have just announced my accident to the entire museum—maybe even to the entire city.

I expect the dinosaur bones will be scattered like stick pretzels, but lucky for me, they aren't. Actually, the raptor skeleton is lying on its side but still completely together.

"Are you OK?" Charlotte offers me a hand up.

Siri and Daisy reach for the raptor and stand it back up. "It must be glued together," Daisy decides.

Charlotte touches the side of the skeleton. "That must be some powerful glue."

"So much for trying to go unnoticed," I mutter. Because just then, Mrs. Sablinsky comes running over.

Jessica picks up the map zippity quick and hides it behind her back.

Mrs. Sablinsky looks concerned. Uh-oh. "What just happened?"

I try to answer the best I can. "I lost my balance. I'm sorry."

Then Mrs. Sablinsky does something super surprising. She actually smiles (with teeth). "I think the dinosaur will be just fine. Are you all right?"

Maybe having your teacher ask you if you are OK is a nice thing. Most of the time, it would be a really nice thing. But it isn't a nice thing when you know you are trying to trick that same teacher and escape from the field trip. Then you get that burning in your cheeks and clench-ing in your stomach like you just got hit with a basketball.

Because you know what you are doing is something that would get you in capital *T* Trouble. You are—

Guilty.

I just nod at my teacher and plaster a fake smile on my face. It will have to do.

"Well then, let's catch up with the rest of the group." Mrs. S gestures for us to go ahead of her. I sigh. This is really not working out the way I planned.

The dinosaur room weaves around, and there are lots of other amazing displays to see. You can even touch a dinosaur bone (which would be a lot more exciting if I hadn't just collided with a whole bunch of bones).

"This is it then," Siri mumbles. She has her worried expression on now, where her eyebrows go down a little and her eyes look super-big. I think I might even spot a single teardrop in the corner of her right eye.

I'm not ready to give up. Not yet.

"There's still time." I squeeze her hand to let her know that I understand.

The funny thing is that sometimes the

thing you think will happen doesn't. And the something else that you didn't think would happen does. Because all of a sudden, without even trying, we have lost the class—or maybe the class has lost us.

Because the five of us are all alone.

"Where did everyone go?" Jessica asks as she gives me the map.

"I don't know." My blurry map can't help us now. I look around the room, but where seconds ago it was filled with students, it is now completely empty. Let me just say that there is a big difference between escaping and being lost.

We are lost.

We run-walk around the same corner that we think the group went around, but they aren't in the shell room. And they aren't in the room after that, which I think is the gem and mineral room. We dash through room after room, just looking for a person we recognize.

That's when I realize what we need to do.

"We can go look for the unicorn clues now without even having to escape."

"What if the bus leaves without us?" Jessica wants to know.

"We have to eat lunch first. There's no way they're leaving yet." Charlotte is the most practical of the five of us.

"We should find the unicorn exhibit," Siri agrees with me.

And that's exactly what we do—well, we try to, anyway. The problem is that we are so turned around that we can't figure out how to get back to the special exhibit area. We go around and around in circles. We see every single room in the museum at least twice, but we can't seem to find Lavender Lakewood's exhibit.

"Did anyone wear a watch?" I ask. It seems like we have been lost for a long time. I don't want to get left here overnight. Reading about running away to a museum is definitely way more fun than experiencing it. The thought of trying to sleep in the bug room makes me sick all over again.

"I did," Jessica answers. She pulls back her sleeve and shows us the watch shaped like a rose. "It's almost noon."

No wonder I'm hungry. All I've had since breakfast are two lemon candies. A museum adventure can really make a girl hungry.

"Can I have one of your granola bars now?" I ask Charlotte. "Nutrition will help me think."

Charlotte hands out the granola bars, and we all sit down on the side of the Pacific Ocean display and bite into the chewy oatmeal bars.

After a few bites, my brain starts working again. There is only one thing to do. But sometimes doing the right thing is harder than it sounds. "I think we should try to find our class." As I say the words out loud, two tears leak out of my eyes and drop down my cheeks like quotation marks. (Every good writer knows her punctuation.)

I guess the Ruby Starr No Crying at School Rule doesn't apply when we aren't actually at school. Or maybe the rule doesn't apply when I know I have let my best friends down and there is absolutely nothing I can do to change it.

"We tried our best." Charlotte puts her arm around Siri's shoulder.

Jessica nudges me with her arm. "We don't even know if we could have found the last unicorn, anyway."

"Experts couldn't even do it," Daisy adds.

"I'll really miss you all," Siri tells us as she looks around at the group. "You are the best friends ever." She takes a big breath like it will help hold in her tears. I can see them shining in her eyes. "Let's find our class."

I point out the window at a white, tentlike structure. "We haven't tried there yet." The five of us hurry to the nearest door. Outside, the sun is shining and a soft breeze is blowing. Somehow, the weather gives me confidence. We peek in the window of the tent.

"There's Will P!" Charlotte calls out.

Siri points at the side of the tent. "I see Mrs. Sablinsky."

And there is our class. We hurry through the double doors into the enclosed garden. As soon as we enter, a blue butterfly glides past me. A yellow butterfly flutters its wings. Mrs. Sablinsky is sitting on a bench covered in butterflies. They are sitting on her head, her shoulders, and even her hands.

"Ruby, you made it. I was getting worried you wouldn't catch up." Mrs. S holds out her hand and an orange monarch flutters onto my arm. "Isn't this wonderful?"

I have to admit that it is pretty wonderful. I also have to admit that if we had found the exhibit, we would have missed this experience completely. Siri is standing with her arms out wide, and butterflies are circling around her. She looks so happy that I know my exhibit wouldn't have matched up to this.

I remember Siri's camera around her wrist. "Want me to take your picture?"

"Can you get it without scaring the butterflies away?" she asks.

"I think so." I gently reach for the strap on Siri's wrist and remove the camera without even frightening away one butterfly.

Then I snap one picture of Siri with matching butterflies on her hair like barrettes and another picture of Siri smiling at the butterfly sitting on her shoulder.

There is one small disruption to this magical scene. That happens when Will B and Bryden get in trouble for chasing the butterflies and trying to catch them in their hands. Will P's mom has to take them outside to the lunch tables early.

Then Jessica, Daisy, and Charlotte sit on a bench with me. Butterflies dance in the air around us. We can't stop laughing.

One thing I know for sure: it's much better to be found than to be lost.

CHAPTER 13

Believing

O nly, that isn't all.

Because Mrs. Sablinsky has another surprise. This one is mostly just for me.

When we leave the butterfly exhibit, she walks us right into a separate room. I see the sign right away: *Lavender Lakewood's Search for Unicorns.*

I turn to my teacher with a huge smile. "This is the best day ever!"

She shrugs as if it's nothing, but we both know this is a super something. "I know how much it meant to you. This might be your last chance to see it." Wait a minute. Mrs. Sablinsky did this just for me? I don't even know what to say—and that doesn't happen to me very often.

The exhibit is tucked into the corner of the room. Golden lights shine down on trees with thick, leafy branches. In the middle of the trees is a small campsite. A wooden folding table and chair covered in papers are in the middle of the campsite. Nearby is a tent with a bed inside. A sketchbook lies open on the table with drawings of unicorns spread out around it. There is even a green jacket with lots of pockets hanging on the back of the chair next to a beige hat. It is made to look as if Lavender just left to search and would be back soon.

On the wall, there is a poster-sized picture of Lavender. It's the same one I saw when Dad and I were doing our research, the one where she looks really sad. Next to the poster is a lot of information about her work. It's mostly information I already know.

Siri grabs my hand. "I can't believe after all that planning Mrs. Sablinsky brought us over to see it."

I grin at my best friend. "I can't believe our escape went so wrong. Claudia must have been much better at running away than we are."

Siri laughs. Jessica joins in. "Any ideas about the message in her writing?"

Now that we are really and truly here, I need to put my sleuthing skills to work. This is the moment I have been waiting for—it's also the moment I have been secretly fearing. I don't want to let my friends down. (Or let myself down either.)

I step closer to look at the open books. The sketches are laid across the pages as if Lavender Lakewood had been looking at them all together.

"Can I use your flashlight?" I say to Jessica.

"Sure." Jessica answers as she takes the little blue flashlight off of her belt loop and hands it to me.

I take a big breath and then hold it as I shine the light over the writing. If the map is hidden in invisible ink, the light should reveal it to us.

Only nothing happens. Nothing at all.

One of my friends behind me sighs and another one lets out a soft "oh" of disappointment. My heart sinks like coins in a wishing well. I thought the map would be there. I was sure of it.

"What about a code?" Siri suggests.

She's right. There could still be a pattern of letters or numbers in the writing. Maybe.

I look at the writing again. I don't see any numbers there. At least nothing that looks like a math equation or a secret code. But then, a secret code wouldn't be secret if everyone could see it. A secret code would have to be hidden.

I imagine Lavender Lakewood sitting right here working on her research. I can see her writing in her notebooks. If I were Lavender, how would I hide the secret?

I know exactly what I would do.

It's a strange idea. And maybe it won't even work.

But it might.

Sometimes it takes imagination to see things other people can't see. You have to see the impossible.

If I'm right, I might just know where the unicorn can be found.

I stand on the edge of Lavender Lakewood's campsite.
Lavender sits in one of the chairs at the table, scribbling in
one of her field journals. Her back is to me, but I can see
that she is wearing her explorer's hat and her jacket with all
the pockets. She doesn't turn around, but she knows I am
here. When she speaks, it is with a British accent, sort of like
my fake one, only real. "Seeking is not always finding. Some
decisions are not ours to make. I know you are wise enough
to understand." I do understand—more than she knows.

"It's time for lunch," Mrs. Sablinsky's voice breaks into my special moment. Why is she always doing that? "Everyone, follow me back to the lunch benches."

I can't leave yet. I need more time. "Can we have a few extra minutes in here?" I paste my most hopeful smile on my face.

The Unicorns catch on right away. This is the amazing thing about best friends: they know you so well that sometimes you don't even have to tell them what you are thinking.

"Please, Mrs. Sablinsky. Just five more minutes?" Charlotte begs.

"Please," Siri, Daisy, and Jessica chorus in harmony.

Mrs. Sablinsky sighs. Then she shrugs. Our teacher shrugs! "How can I resist all of these puppy-dog eyes? Five minutes. Meet us just outside that door. Please, do not get lost."

"We won't," I promise. My friends look at me and grin. Getting lost is our specialty.

As soon as the rest of the class leaves the room, I step closer to the table. Seeing the sketch laid on the side of the written notes makes me think of a poetry exercise Mrs. Sablinsky had us try in class one time. We drew a shape in pencil and then filled it in with words to describe the shape. When it was filled with words, we erased the outside line. The words formed the shape.

"I want to try something," I tell my friends. "Remember that poetry assignment with the shapes?"

I pull my pen and sheets of paper out of my shirt pocket. Then I climb into the exhibit and sit down in the chair. I'll have to be extra careful not to knock anything over in this exhibit. My friends gather around.

"You might get in trouble for being in there," Daisy warns.

She's right, of course. But I haven't come all

this way to give up now. "If someone comes, I'll climb out superfast."

I lay my paper next to the first book and carefully copy one of Lavender's unicorn drawings. Then I open to the first page of the field guide. There, I see what I am looking for. A shiver of excitement slides down the back of my neck. This must be how Nancy Drew feels when she is about to solve a mystery: like everything is falling into place.

I know what we need to do next. "Can you help me tear out the middle of the shape?"

I hand my friends the paper with the unicorn drawing. Then we take turns carefully tearing out the middle of the unicorn along the lines I have drawn.

When Daisy tears out the last piece, we have an empty unicorn cut out in the middle of my wrinkled paper. "Perfect!" I place the open shape over the words in the journal. It turns out that the words outside the shape are camouflage for the secret message inside the unicorn. I hold up the book so everyone can see. We read it out loud together:

If you are a true unicorn seeker you will leave the unicorn in peace. Some would seek to destroy these majestic creatures. They are hidden away and only reveal themselves to the most worthy when the time is right. May you always Believe.

"We solved the mystery, but what does it mean?" Charlotte asks.

Our search led us to the answer—but not to the unicorn.

"If we want to keep the last unicorn safe, we have to leave it hidden." I look at my friends. "We can't become famous Unicorn Seekers after all."

"But we did something even the experts couldn't do," Jessica points out. "That's pretty amazing."

Siri says the thing the rest of us are all thinking but are too afraid to say out loud. "We won't be famous though."

We won't be famous. Because to be famous, we would be hurting the last hidden unicorn.

"It's not fair," Daisy whispers. "We know the answer, but we can't tell anyone about it."

I step out of the exhibit and join my friends. "Lavender is asking us to keep the secret."

We all know that keeping the secret means we will have to say goodbye to Siri.

Standing in Lavender's forest, I know that this is not the last adventure the Unicorns will have together. I don't know how I know this. I just do.

On the day my book report is due, I begin my presentation standing in front of the class next to my poster about Lavender Lakewood. I have printed out the photo and then sketched my own version of her campsite. I have also written out some important sentences from her research.

"She was a brave adventurer who discovered the last unicorn. Then she wrote two books about her research. She hid the secret about the unicorn in her work so that no one could find it. Well, no one except true Unicorn Seekers."

I look over at Mrs. Sablinsky, who nods at me. She has already approved my surprise.

"I would like to ask the other Unicorn Seekers to present this last part with me. Siri, Jessica, Daisy, and Charlotte, could you please come up here?"

My friends come to the front of the room. We

all stand side by side. Here's the order: me, Siri, Charlotte, Jessica, and Daisy.

I hand each one a present I have made for them. It's a lavender, braided friendship bracelet with a silver unicorn charm in the middle.

"Thank you for your courage and for believing in the unicorn," I say in my most official-sounding voice. "You will forever be Unicorn Seekers."

Everyone claps after that. I can't believe my eyes or my ears—Mrs. Sablinsky claps the loudest!

I know Siri and I won't be together every day at school. And I will probably cry a few (or a lot) more tears over it. But we will always be Unicorns. Like my brother said: Who knows what will happen in the future?

Things might even turn out exactly the way we planned.

Siri and I are finally living in New York City. There are tall buildings all around us, but our apartment is actually inside a house-sized red apple. Siri has dress forms everywhere, and I am writing a novel on a very long sheet of paper that keeps going and going. Buddy the fox lives with us. Outside the apple, a unicorn peeks in the window. I stopped looking for the unicorn, but it seems the unicorn never stopped looking for me.

You can learn anything from books. One thing I learned is that friendship lasts forever.

Acknowledgements

To readers, parents, teachers, and librarians, thank you for reading and sharing my book! I hope you enjoyed Ruby's latest adventure.

I am so grateful to all the people who have helped make this book possible.

To my agent, Stacey Glick, thank you for being Ruby's champion from the beginning. I truly appreciate your support and friendship. To my editor, Annie Berger, thank you for your vision and guidance. It is a joy to work with someone who loves stories as much as I do! To my copy editor, Lauren Dombrowski, thank you for working so hard on this book and for helping me to make it the best it could be. To Nicole Hower and Jordan Kost, thank you for creating such adorable Ruby designs that flow right from the words themselves. To Sarah Kasman, thank you for your focus on this manuscript so it would be fabulously fabulous. To Jeanine Murch, illustrator extraordinaire, you have captured every one of Ruby's thoughts so perfectly—thank you! To Stefani Sloma, my PR and marketing BFF, thank you so much for your enthusiasm and professionalism. To Margaret Coffee, thank you for all of your efforts to get Ruby out to schools and libraries! To Dominique Raccah, Todd Stocke, and Steve Geck, thank you for your commitment to this series and for encouraging imagination and freedom of ideas in all of your Sourcebooks writers.

To my family, thank you for your prayers and for always encouraging me to follow my dreams.

To my daughters, Ava and Caroline, thank you for all your help from visiting bookstores to shooting my head shots. Most of all, thank you for inspiring me every single day.

To Jesus, thank you for everything.

About the Author

Deborah Lytton writes books for middle grade and young adult readers. She is the author of *Jane in Bloom* and *Silence*. Deborah has a history degree from UCLA and a law degree from Pepperdine University. She lives in Los Angeles, California, with her two daughters and their dog, Faith. For more information about Deborah, visit deborahlytton.com.

Read on for the start
to Ruby's story in

CHAPTER 1

It All Begins with Books

*O*nce upon a time opens every fairy tale so it's the way I'm starting my own story. Once upon a time, there lived a girl named Ruby Starr. (That's me.) Here are some things you should know:

1. I love—absolutely, completely *love*—books (every kind of book, especially if it involves animals).

2. Pickles are my favorite food. (They go with everything. Even chocolate ice cream! Hmm, this is making me hungry...)

3. I say a lot of things without thinking

(which sometimes gets me in trouble with a lowercase *t*).

4. The book that made me love books was *Harry Potter and the Sorcerer's Stone*. (Probably everyone says that, right?)

5. I have three besties—Siri, Jessica, and Daisy.

6. Sometimes I imagine I am in the pages of a book. My thoughts sort of fly up into bubble-gum bubbles full of ideas.

7. I believe in happy endings.

Today I'm not imagining things when my teacher, Mrs. Sablinsky, announces that we will be welcoming a new student to Room 15. (This is the way lots of books begin—with someone new coming to town.) I sit up a little taller in my seat and glance across the room at my best friend, Siri

Mundy. Siri and I have been best friends since we were in kindergarten. Kindergarten to fifth grade is a lifetime. So we have been friends for something like forever. Siri raises her eyebrows and grins back at me. She just got braces, and they make her smile look even happier than usual.

I know what Siri is thinking. 'Cause I'm thinking the same thing. Someone new to join our Fearsome Foursome: Siri, Jessica, Daisy, and yours truly. (There's nothing really fearsome about us at all. I just like to say that because it sounds sort of superheroish.) Pink is our signature color. We use pink markers whenever possible, wear pink clips in our hair, and have pink laces in our sneakers. Even Siri's braces are pink. Confession time: I like green better than pink, but I got outvoted. So I wear the pink, but in my heart, I'm all about the green.

I watch the door all morning. It's not that easy to write in cursive with my eyes looking up instead of down at my paper. But when a new character is about to step into the pages of a story, you don't want to miss it. I want to be the very first person in Room 15 to see who it is. Finally, the star-spangly door opens. She looks like she is already one of our group. She wears a pink headband in her smooth black hair, a floral skirt with a white tank top, and pink sneakers. She also looks sort of nervous, if you ask me. I think of all the books I've read about new kids, like Harry Potter, coming into a story. They always turn out to be the heroes. I'm not sure I like that.

"Class, this is Charlotte Thomas. Charlotte has just moved here from Northern California. I want everyone to welcome her and help her get settled in." Charlotte stands there quietly. But her eyes dart around the room. *Look at me, look at me!* I scream silently. Only her eyes skip right over me to land on Siri. I glance over at my best friend. Siri is smiling at Charlotte with her sparkly braces. Charlotte suddenly smiles back. And I can't believe my eyes. She has the same pink braces as Siri! Something in my stomach flips over right then. I know, somehow, that there is trouble ahead (maybe even trouble with a capital *T*).

So when Mrs. Sablinsky says, "Who would like to show Charlotte around and sit with her at lunch today?" I keep my eyes on Siri and raise my hand as fast as she raises hers. Only I must be faster, because Mrs. Sablinsky picks me. "Thank you, Ruby. I'm counting on you to make Charlotte's first day really special."

When Mrs. Sablinsky starts going over the schedule for the rest of the day, I begin imagining things.

I see myself walking Charlotte down a pink carpet. The other students stand along the carpet, taking photos of us like we are famous. The carpet leads all the way around school. Even Principal Snyder is waving to us. I wave back like a princess on parade. Only I don't see my glass slipper fall off. And I trip over it and tumble down the stairs, landing with a splash in a river of pickles.

"Ruby, did you have a question?" Mrs. Sablinsky's voice cuts into my imaginary world and drops me right back into the present. I want to say no, but my hand is waving back and forth in the air as though I have a very important question to ask. I don't want to embarrass myself, so I make one up, really fast. "What time is it in Paris?"

OK, it's not my best question. It's not even my sort-of-best question. It's lame. So I deserve the snickers and giggles. Even I want to giggle.

"Not amusing, Ruby." Mrs. Sablinsky does not have a sense of humor. I bet if a line of dancing goats came into the room right now wearing ballet tutus, she wouldn't even crack a smile. If you ask me, a sense of humor should be a requirement for teaching degrees. If I made the test for teachers, they would have to show that they can laugh at jokes and play charades. I'm positively one hundred percent certain that Mrs. Sablinsky hasn't ever played charades. (Charades is one of my top three favorite games:

1. Chess
2. Monopoly
3. Charades)

The class is still laughing at me. I look over at Siri and shrug. I pretend it's no big deal, but truthfully, I hate when people laugh at me. I love laughing. And I love jokes too. I just don't want to be one.

I keep my eyes on my work after that. I don't allow my mind to wander once. Then I hear the bell ring. Everyone around me scrambles out of their seats and runs for the door. I stand slowly and walk over to Charlotte. I don't want to seem too anxious. But Siri beats me there.